Convincing

Cami

His Girl Next Door - Book 2

by

Babette James

Chara Press

CONVINCING CAMI

Cover Design and Interior Design by Jamie Banta
Images from Depositphotos.com

Chara Press
PO Box 281
Keasbey, NJ 08832

Visit Babette at www.BabetteJames.com

Publishing History
First Edition, 2015
Print ISBN-13: 978-0-9862513-2-0

Printed in the United States of America

THE OLD WOODEN LADDER CREAKED AND ROCKED WITH loose joints as Cami climbed. The thing must be as old as the house. She stretched, screwing in the first bulb. The step under her feet creaked, cracked—

And gave way. She shrieked, dropping the light bulb, but grabbed only air. Oh, this was going to hurt—

"Cami!" Jack shouted. Strong arms clamped around her. "I got you."

Shaken from the close call, she melted into him. "Thanks. That was too close."

"I knew I should've brought my ladders over. You okay?"

"Yes. Just a scare."

He let her slide to the floor, but held her snug against his body. He would release her, any second now. She should step away. Instead, she wrapped her arms around his waist. She shivered, this time less from the scare and more from realizing just how close he held her. How he'd never actually touched her before beyond a social hug or handshake.

Her quiet little crush speared into a hot rush of want. How warm and sturdy he was. How perfectly they fit together.

She caught her breath and looked up to find Jack studying her with a puzzled, serious expression that she'd never seen on his face before. The twilight added a deceptive privacy to the dim room and made Jack's eyes appear dark and deep with—

Desire?

"This is a really bad idea," Jack muttered. Tightening his arms, he crushed his mouth down on hers.

Praise for Babette James

Summertime Dream

Summertime Dream is a perfect glass of Lemonade on a hot day. Simple, elegant and beautifully written. I enjoyed each scene. Loved the chemistry between the characters and the house. Great story! ~ Deborah Diez

Family is of utmost importance in life for both characters in spite of their vastly different backgrounds. This makes their instant connection and love of solving a family mystery so enjoyable to follow. Their love of, and dedication to, fixing the house is a beautiful metaphor on the work relationships take . . . ~ InD'Tale Magazine (4½ Stars–Crowned Heart)

I loved this story! The unveiling of the house in all its ancient glory was quite interesting to read, and equally as intriguing as the mystery of Christopher's family genealogy. I thought this plot line was quite unique and unfolded in a well written and engaging way. The romance between Christopher and Margie was sweet and tender and developed at just the right pace. The overall story was a fun, lighthearted read filled with tender moments and emotionally satisfying scenes. 5 delightful stars! ~ Maria Rose for RomCon Reader

Loved this sweet and sexy small town romance! Totally Recommend and Will Definitely look for more stories from Babette James! The scenes between Christopher and Margie range from sweet to steamy, and the secondary characters all add so much to the story. ~ Katie O'Sullivan

Clear As Day

I truly loved how Ms. James expressed so well the emotional rollercoaster of their relationship. The fears, happiness, confusion and pain that Kay went through in coming to a decision of her next step to this relationship was expressed wonderfully. This book truly made me laugh, giggle and cry. ~ The Romance Reviews (5 Stars–Top Pick)

I loved not only the love story this book offered, but the dynamic of the side characters as well. I also fell in love with the emotional roller coaster this book took me on. ~ Insightful Minds Reviews

Though very sensual, this is still a sweet romance. ~ Romantic Times Book Reviews (4½ Stars)

Kissing Katie

What a lovely story! I was particularly entranced by the setting detail in the first chapter - the sights and smells of the beach setting were so vivid that it was easy to picture and added to the delight of Matt reliving his childhood memories and finding his old friend Kate still there. I loved how their romance progressed, with a new sexual attraction as adults combined with good memories of their friendship. Overall it was a pure delight to read. 5 stars! ~ Maria Rose

~*~

Books by Babette James

The River Series
Summertime Dream
Clear As Day

His Girl Next Door Series
Kissing Katie
Convincing Cami

Dedicated to

Margie

Thanks for all your encouragement and being a loving slave driver in chat!

~*~

O hushed October morning mild,
Begin the hours of this day slow,
Make the day seem to us less brief.
Hearts not averse to being beguiled,
Beguile us in the way you know;
Release one leaf at break of day;
At noon release another leaf;
One from our trees, one far away;
Retard the sun with gentle mist;
Enchant the land with amethyst.
Slow, slow!

Robert Frost, *October*

~*~

Chapter One

*C*OME ON, CAMI, THIS IS TOTALLY PERFECT, RIGHT?"
Cami Alexander wrinkled her nose at the tidy,
but old fixer-upper that had her twin sister
Mikki in a tizzy.

Mikki rattled on breathlessly, her brown eyes
shining. "I mean, this is meant to be. We wanted to
stay in Point Pleasant, and what are the odds that
the only mother-daughter house on our street comes
on the market the same day you hear you need to
find a new apartment?"

"We'll see. Let's go on inside, get you out of the
heat, and take a look." Cami caught Mikki's elbow
and nudged her along the walk to the front porch.
Her very pregnant sister didn't need to be standing
in the sun on this hot August day.

Sighing dreamily, Mikki nodded. "I've coveted
this property for five years now, ever since we first

rented our little cottage. This is totally my dream house. Say you'll go in on this with us, please."

"It's a cute place, but . . ."

Cami's resolve was already cracking. She needed a new apartment, she'd rather pay rent to Mikki than a stranger, she was tired of fighting traffic to and from school, and she wanted to live closer to Mikki. Most importantly, Mikki adored this sprawling two-story house.

"You haven't even been inside yet. How can you be so sure?"

Mikki glowed with anticipation. "I know, I just know." She swept an arm around the porch. "Ray already said if you agree, he'll make the offer today. Jack knew the owners, the Palmers. He's friends with their son Wayne and has been looking after the place since Wayne moved to Austin. Jack says it's in good shape inside—and Ray trusts Jack when it comes to houses. We've been looking around town for ages, and this is the perfect one for us. Emily would keep her friends, and I love this neighborhood and all my neighbors. Jack would be our next-door neighbor, which is simply terrific for Ray."

Mikki patted her belly, round with her growing twin girls. "Best of all, we'll finally have room for all the girls. Since it's an estate sale, it's possible we could be closed, moved, and settled in two months or less—just in time for Christie and Kaylie's arrival. You'd be near me, you'll save money on rent, and you could even walk to school if you want. Say yes, pretty please?"

Someone had to be sensible about this. Mikki was too in love with the house. Only . . . the house being about a mile from the elementary school where she taught was a huge temptation.

Cami steeled herself. "I'm not promising anything until we've walked through the whole property. And even if Jack knows the house, you still need a home inspection. There could be foundation issues, electrical problems, or termites. What if it needs a new roof?"

"Don't worry! Thank you! I know you'll love it too."

Two hours later, after strolling around and peering into practically every square inch of house and yard, Mikki gave her those wide brown puppy eyes. "Well? What do you think? Tell me you love the house as much as I do."

The spacious main house was perfect for her sister's growing family. Shady oaks and maples sheltered the property. The huge yard, deck, and patio held plenty of room for children to play in and to hold the parties Mikki and Ray loved to throw, and a sunny grassy stretch and a small raised-bed vegetable garden set off by an old wire fence lay behind the two-car garage.

As for the space that would be Cami's, the two-bedroom, bath-and-a-half apartment was nearly as big as Mikki's rental down the street and enormous compared to her current apartment, with a full-sized kitchen and living room. A wide breezeway with louvered windows connected the two buildings and would make a nice sun porch.

Cami caved. "I'm in. I think it's perfect too."

With a joyful squeal, Mikki crushed Cami in an exuberant hug. "Thank you, thank you! This will be the most perfect thing. Just you wait and see. I'm going to call Ray now."

"Sit down, drink your water, and rest your feet while you do." She pressed Mikki toward the nearest front porch chair.

"Good idea." Mikki lowered herself with a groan, and swept back her blonde bangs. "Oh, what was I thinking? Pregnant through the summer? I'm going to be a whale by the time October arrives."

"If Mom could do it, you can too."

"So she tells me every day." Mikki gave a wincing smile.

"Okay, while you talk to Ray, I'm going to wander through the apartment again."

"Have fun. And start thinking how you want to decorate and begin a shopping list of things you'll want and need. We're going to have so much fun!"

And a lot of work, but Cami kept that thought to herself as she followed the slate walk to the apartment's front door.

She glanced beyond the low, neatly trimmed privet hedge running along the property line to the sage green ranch house belonging to Ray's best friend, Jack O'Malley. She'd been to countless barbecues and parties at his house over the years, and she liked his more modern and upgraded home.

However, as for living next door to Jack O'Malley . . .

That should prove interesting. She'd always had the tiniest crush on Jack from day one of meeting him, but she'd never had an opportunity to act on the attraction. If she wasn't in a relationship, Jack was, and vice versa. On top of life's poor timing over the last six years, he'd never shown any interest in her that way, treating her as he treated Mikki:

simple good friends, as if she were Ray's off-limits sister rather than available sister-in-law.

And speak of the devil.

Jack's red SUV with kayak strapped on the rack pulled into the driveway. He jumped out of the truck and waved, kicking off that usual, useless, hot thrill.

"Hi, Cami. Did Mikki like the house?" He strolled over to the hedge. Well, no complaints about the view next door when it came to Jack and his dark good looks, wide smile, and piercing, pale blue eyes. A day-old beard shadowed his jaw today, and thanks to his kayak outing, he only wore swim trunks and sandals on his appealing, fit body.

"Mikki's head over heels in love. She's talking to Ray right now." Oh, living next door to Jack was going to be more awkward than interesting if her pulse kept rushing every time he smiled.

"Awesome. When Wayne gave me the heads up, I had to tell Ray the place was available."

"If home ownership could happen by sheer force of will, this place is hers already."

"I'm sure Wayne and Ray can work out a deal. Wayne liked the idea of selling without needing a real estate agent. I hope Ray and Mikki can find a good tenant for the apartment."

Cami grinned. "Already solved. Me." She was feeling better and better about the decision.

His gorgeous eyes widened. "Hey, that's great! Mikki must be in seventh heaven. But I thought you were happy in your place."

"I love my apartment, but my landlady is selling, and I just found out I have to move. Toms River isn't all that far away, but I really want to live close to

Mikki again, especially now with the twins coming. She'll need me."

"Solves the commuting problem."

"Definitely. I'll miss my bay view, but I'm looking forward to walking to work on nice days."

"Fingers crossed for you all on the deal working out." He flashed that smile again.

She ignored the warm, but useless flutter in her middle. "Thanks."

Her phone rang, and a peek at the caller ID showed Brent was calling from work when he should be on the road south already. Her heart sank. This would not be a 'Do you want me to pick up wine' call.

"I'll let you answer that. See you later." Jack waved and headed back to his truck.

After a frustrated groan aimed at both men and herself, she answered the call. "Hi, Brent."

"Hi, Cami. I have to cancel our plans for the weekend. Sorry, I know I swore nothing would get in the way this time, but Giselle flew in, and now I'll be stuck in the office with the team all weekend getting ready to head back to Anaheim. I already cancelled all our reservations."

"Okay." She sighed. One more promise broken in a string of broken promises.

"Sorry again. Got to run. I'll call you later, okay?"

"Sure, but just one thing before you go—" She spoke to a disconnected call. He'd hung up without giving her a chance to share her house and apartment news.

Déjà vu all over again, as Dad liked to quote. Brent was so distant lately, blaming work, but she could see the writing on the wall. They barely saw each other anymore. What was wrong with her that she couldn't make a relationship work?

She slipped her phone into her purse. On the bright side, now she was free to spend the rest of the day with Mikki and Emily.

"Cami!" Mikki called out jubilantly. "Ray's calling Wayne now. Fingers crossed."

Tucking her heartache away, Cami grinned and crossed her fingers.

~*~

"Jack, we got the keys! The closing's over. The house is ours!" Ray's elated voice boomed through Jack's cell phone.

Jack groaned under his breath. Heaven help him, Cami Alexander was officially his neighbor. For two months now, he'd been anticipating and dreading this day.

"Congratulations."

"Come on over. We're having takeout there tonight out on the deck. We just pulled into the driveway."

"I'll bring the beer." He gritted his teeth. Slim chance of Cami having other plans. With Mikki's due date rapidly approaching, she'd been glued to Mikki's side.

Please, please, don't let the boyfriend be there.

Keeping his cool distance on the frequent social gatherings and meals together was hard enough, but now he'd likely be seeing her every day—and see her welcome her boyfriend through her door.

"Great. See you in a few." Ray hung up.

Jack banged his head against the fridge door. Once more into the breach.

He grabbed the beer, champagne, and sparkling

cider he had ready in the fridge along with the plastic glasses, and headed for the door.

They had a beautiful, warm October evening, and the forecast for the next several days was for clear skies and Indian summer heat after the last few days of early autumn chill.

Mikki was already sitting in one of the patio chairs on the deck, looking hugely uncomfortable with the coming twins, but her smile was beaming. Ray said all was great with the pregnancy, and they were cautiously optimistic about reaching their November 10th due date, or least clearing Halloween.

He grinned at three-year-old Emily, who was bouncing in circles around the table with a new doll, and definitely dancing to her own drummer in her fairy princess outfit and red cowboy boots.

"Hi, Mikki. You look happy."

"I'm bouncing like Emily on the inside. Thank you so much for your perfect housewarming gift! The cleaning company you hired did a great job. The place practically sparkles."

"You're welcome."

"Unca Jack!" Emily scampered over to him and hugged his leg. "We gotta new house."

"Hey, neighbor." Ray stepped out the kitchen door, followed by Cami, both laden with take-out bags.

Jack set down the bottles. "Hey, neighbor yourself. Congratulations again, all of you."

As his excited friends bubbled over with the story of their day, he poured champagne for Ray, Cami, and himself and the cider for Mikki and Emily.

He raised his glass. "Here's to you all, my good

friends, and may you have many wonderful years in your new home."

"Hear, hear!"

As Jack drank, he studied Cami and Mikki. The sisters were pretty damned close in looks. Both had long, pale blonde hair, soft rosy lips, and big, brown bedroom eyes. Cami was slightly taller and Mikki, when not pregnant, was a hair curvier. Cami was more reserved and Mikki more bubbly. Strange how, when he first met Mikki six years ago when she began dating Ray, he'd thought her nice, but the moment he met Cami, an electrifying charge of desire had smacked him flat.

Unfortunately, Cami and he'd both been in relationships at the time, or he might have investigated that attraction then and there. Their timing had stayed messed up ever since. Like now, he was unattached, but she was dating Brent. Six years later, that undying attraction remained an uncomfortable companion, however firmly repressed.

On top of bad timing issues, he'd always worried if they did date and things went sour, that chanced ruining his friendship with them all. They'd slipped into a family-type relationship and good friends were far harder to find than a fun date for the weekend.

"So, Jack, still good for tomorrow?"

Ray's question knocked Jack out of his mulling. "Huh?"

"Are you still good for helping with the move tomorrow?"

"Yes. Schedule's totally clear through the weekend."

Emily clambered onto the picnic bench beside

Jack. "Unca Jack, you gonna build my big girl princess bed?"

He ruffled Emily's blond fluff of curls. "Sure will. Anything for my favorite princess."

"Aunt Cami gotta new bed too, so you gotta build hers too. Aunt Cami says Daddy's got too many plates."

Ray and Mikki laughed.

Cami blushed. "I can certainly put my own bed together."

More likely Brent would be the one helping. He was a nice enough guy for a workaholic, with a decent sense of humor. Strange that he wasn't here to join in the celebration.

Might as well put the question head on. "Is Brent coming by tonight?"

"Nuh uh," Emily piped up, a hurt pout on her face. "No more Mr. Brent. He got transfurtered to Angel Land. Mr. Brent likes angels better'n us."

What?

Cami winced and rolled her eyes. "Translation is Brent got a great promotion and was transferred permanently to his firm's headquarters in Los Angeles. We agreed to break up." She sipped at her champagne.

"Ah, gee, I'm sorry." He managed to sound sympathetic, considering his heart and libido were jumping in excited shock.

Holy shit! Cami was unattached. He was finally free and clear to discover if there could be more between them than friends.

"All I have to say is Brent better not show his face around here again," Ray growled.

"Really, Ray, it's okay. I'm totally fine." Cami's

gaze slipped aside and she shrugged. "Brent and I simply fizzled out, you know? His traveling so much made staying connected difficult. Honestly, I was relieved. I want someone who's always around, like Mikki has with you."

Mikki threw her arms around Cami. "Aw, sis, you'll find the perfect guy for you. Just you wait."

Cami smiled thinly. "So, who's hungry?"

"Meee!" Emily bounced in her seat.

Ray and Jack unpacked the fried chicken, fries, and coleslaw, while Cami handed around paper plates and forks.

Jack refilled glasses and tried to stay intelligently involved in the conversation despite his mind spinning from the news. He could be that perfect guy for Cami. All he needed was a chance.

Mikki arranged Emily's chicken fingers and fries on the plate. "I wish we could sleep here tonight. I know you can hardly wait to get off our couch and sleep in your own bed again, Cami."

"Very true, but at least your couch is comfortable. I bet Jack will be happy to have our stuff out of his garage."

Cami had vacated her apartment back in September and had been staying with Ray and Mikki in their tiny place. Everything she owned filled Jack's garage, along with all the new nursery furniture and other deliveries for Ray and Mikki's house.

"Hey, I'm just glad I had the space and could help out." He selected a chicken leg and passed the bucket to Ray. "I have an idea. It's early enough, how about Ray and I start bringing things over from my garage? Mikki can relax and supervise."

"I can set up the bed frames," Cami offered.

Mikki sighed. "I want to do something. I'm feeling great. I'm too excited to be tired. I'd love to get started."

"Hon, how about I cart over some of the kitchen boxes? You can unwrap, and I'll put the stuff on the shelves and in the drawers. You and your mom can reorganize them tomorrow." Ray grinned.

Mikki brightened. "Oh, that would be great. Unpacking is easy to do while sitting, and Emily can have fun helping. And if I do feel tired, there's a very comfy sofa to put my feet up."

Once they'd demolished the fried chicken, Ray and he drove over to Ray's rental and loaded up four boxes from the kitchen.

"Hey, Ray? Cami and Brent, they're really split?"

Ray stopped and narrowed his eyes at Jack. "Yeah, why?"

Okay, not playing things cool enough. "Just worried about Cami. I hate to see her hurt, you know?"

"Yeah, Cami's great." Ray sighed. "Brent seemed nice enough in the beginning, but Mikki said she always knew it wasn't going to work. I know Cami said she was fine when Brent broke the transfer news to her, but she was really hurt. Mikki's pretty sure the jerk was also screwing around with that new boss of his too. He didn't even have the balls to break the news face-to-face. He emailed her from California after he'd relocated."

"Damn. What a shitass move." Jack clenched his fist behind his back, his heart aching for Cami.

"Yeah. I want to beat the crap out of him." He slammed the truck hatch closed. "I'm really sick of these guys playing around with Cami's feelings, raising her hopes, and then dropping her. I want her to meet someone who really gets her, who's really into her, and wants to have a family. Brent also never really understood the whole twin closeness thing between Cami and Mikki. He always acted like Mikki took too much of Cami's time. Which is bullshit, considering he never had time for Cami. A guy should put effort into making his girl or wife first in his life, right? Cami deserves a guy who won't screw around or slither out of her life when things get serious or difficult."

Jack mulled all that over. He got the whole closeness thing between the sisters. As an only child, he thought their tight friendship was great, actually. He wanted a family. He was definitely into Cami.

Now, the hard part: discovering if Cami could feel the same for him.

~*~

While she waited for Ray and Jack to deliver the bed parts, Cami unloaded the cleaning and painting supplies and tools from her car, along with all the new curtain rods, curtains, bed linens, and down pillows.

Done with that, she checked on Mikki and found her happily settled in the living room unwrapping packing paper with Emily setting the objects on the coffee table and hearth, while the soundtrack from *The Little Mermaid* blared from the DVD player.

Emily held up salad tongs. "Aunt Cami! Look! I'm a helper!"

"Yes, you are. Can I get anything for you, Mikki, while I'm here?"

"Emily and I are good. I'm sorry again, about Brent."

"I'm really okay. We hardly saw each other over the past months. It's almost like we broke up back in July rather than September."

"If you need to talk, I'm here for you, sis. Any time."

"Thanks." She hugged Mikki. "So, how does it feel to be a homeowner?"

"Absolutely wonderful." Mikki glanced joyfully around the living room. "And I'm so happy the house came with all this furniture. We never could have afforded to furnish the place on our own all at once like this. It's perfect!"

"It's all kind of old." Perfect, maybe, decades ago when the mostly Fifties and Sixties era furniture was new.

"True, but most of the pieces are in great shape and were high quality when new. You know how I love the old-fashioned, retro look. I've seen pieces like these in the antique stores around town and online, and they're worth something. Even better, it's real wood. I can refinish and reupholster the shabbier pieces little by little." Mikki beamed. "My own house. I can paint and make it all perfectly ours. Can you see that mantle all decorated for Christmas over a crackling fire, ready for sitting with hot cocoa and warming up after playing outside on a snowy day?"

Cami easily pictured Mikki's dream. The big fireplace had a wide mantel and a lovely tiled hearth, perfect for displaying Mikki's antique decorations. "The room will be beautiful."

"I can't wait for Gerry and Claire and the kids to see the place. And we have room for them to stay with us! I miss them so much. A two-week visit with them for Thanksgiving won't be nearly long enough."

"I know what you mean."

Their older brother Gerry and his family had relocated to Alaska for his job four years ago and between his work schedule and the long distance, seeing them as often as they wanted was tough.

The doorbell chimed crazily, and then the guys carried in the mattress for Emily's new bed, laughing and joking.

The look of love for Ray in Mikki's face drove a lonely ache through Cami's chest.

Mikki turned back to Cami. "When you're ready to date again, you should look for someone different than Brent. Really. You should make a list of traits you want in a man."

"Hmm, you think?" Struck with a flush of warmth, Cami paused, appreciating how appealing Jack looked in those snug, old jeans and how his shoulders flexed as he hoisted the bottom end of the mattress.

"I did. And I stuck to my list and found Ray. Fun, kind, smart, handy with tools, and oh, so easy on the eyes." Mikki grinned at the two men guiding the mattress up the staircase.

And her sister was also eyeing Jack's jean-clad rear.

"Mikki!"

"Hey, I'm allowed to appreciate the view."

"It is a very nice view."

When the men came downstairs, Cami and Mikki glanced from them to each other and burst into a fit of giggles.

Jack gave a puzzled smile.

Ray just stared and shook his head. "Cami, we're doing your bed next. Want to show us which room?"

After delivering her mattress and frame parts, Ray left to load the truck.

Jack paused and ran a hand over headboard's curving iron rail. "Real nice bed frame. Want help putting this together?"

When she'd moved out of her apartment, she'd decided the time had come to stop making do and buy the bed she wanted, so she'd chosen a gorgeous wrought iron and oak bedframe and a lusciously soft queen mattress set.

"No, but thanks, I really appreciate you bringing everything upstairs. I have this under control. You can go ahead and work on Emily's bed."

"Okay, just give a shout if you need anything."

Her bedframe proved easy to assemble, and she soon had the box spring and mattress stacked in place. She pulled the new sheet set from the bag. She'd already washed them, and the silky cotton smelled fresh and cozy.

After fitting the mattress cover and the bottom sheet, the urge to check out the mattress was irresistible. She threw herself laughing onto the cushy bed. Her new home was going to work out wonderfully.

Cami stretched out on her back, feet hanging over the edge. She couldn't wait to sleep here in her own peaceful, private space. Technically, she could tonight, but Mikki might feel left out, so she'd wait until tomorrow. Anyhow, Mom and Dad were coming at the crack of dawn tomorrow to help with the move, and Mikki and she had plans for a big family breakfast to start the day. Happily, Mikki's couch was very comfortable.

A light bulb blew in the ceiling fan high overhead, leaving only one functioning bulb out of three, but she had enough light to finish making the bed. Time to get back to work. She pushed to her feet and shook out the top sheet.

The last bulb blinked out, dousing her in dim twilight.

Rats. Time for new bulbs and she'd need a ladder to reach the fixture.

After fetching fresh bulbs from her kitchen, she lugged in the ladder from the breezeway.

The old wooden ladder creaked and rocked with loose joints as Cami climbed. The thing must be as old as the house. She stretched, screwing in the first bulb. The step under her feet creaked, cracked—

And gave way. She shrieked, dropping the light bulb, but grabbed only air. Oh, this was going to hurt—

"Cami!" Jack shouted. Strong arms clamped around her. "I got you."

Shaken from the close call, she melted into him. "Thanks. That was too close."

"I knew I should've brought my ladders over. You okay?"

"Yes. Just a scare."

He let her slide to the floor, but held her snug against his body. He would release her, any second now. She should step away. Instead, she wrapped her arms around his waist. She shivered, this time less from the scare and more from realizing just how close he held her. How he'd never actually touched her before beyond a social hug or handshake.

Her quiet little crush speared into a hot rush of want. How warm and sturdy he was. How perfectly they fit together.

She caught her breath and looked up to find Jack studying her with a puzzled, serious expression that she'd never seen on his face before. The twilight added a deceptive privacy to the dim room and made Jack's eyes appear dark and deep with—

Desire?

"This is a really bad idea," Jack muttered. Tightening his arms, he crushed his mouth down on hers.

She gasped, and he seized full advantage of her mouth opening under his in the hungry, demanding kiss.

Oh, Jack was right, this was a really bad idea, but the surprising kiss was far too amazing to rally any effort to break away. With the curiosity of six years pressing her, Cami recklessly surrendered to the pleasure, not caring he had a girlfriend, not caring they'd just careened over the friendship line . . . and his warm body was hard against hers.

What a kiss! Far from a perfect kiss—too hot and rushed—but wonderful, wonderful, fierce, and toe-curling.

Curiosity killed the cat, remember.

Well, she wasn't a cat, and this was just a kiss. Right?

Chapter Two

⭐

JACK DRAGGED HIS MOUTH FROM CAMI'S, DAZED
with desire, his heart pounding, his world
rocked by the kiss.

Oh, shit, that kiss had gotten out of hand, but
wow . . .

"Sorry." He peeled his hands from her and took
two cautious steps back. Maybe if he pleaded shock
from seeing that ladder step snap and her falling.

Cami caught a steadying hand on the ladder, so
gorgeous in the shadowy light and looking as
thunderstruck as he felt, her brown eyes wide and
deep.

"Look, I'm really sorry."

Cami shivered. "Ah, no, it's okay. The moment,
you know, just happened. Thanks, uh, for catching
me."

"Right. The moment." That and holding her

close, her soft body pressed to his, his body charged and ready for more than kissing . . .

He made himself step away and pick up the broken light bulb. "This one's toast. You'll need a dustpan."

Oh, that's inane.

An unbroken bulb lay caught in the gap between mattress and footboard. A fresh, intense rush of awareness slammed him. If only things were different. He could be still kissing Cami, backing her up to that very comfortable bed . . .

Holy shit, he needed to pull his mind off of the bed.

He carefully used the rickety ladder to replace the dead bulb with the unbroken one. Light flooded the room.

She shouldn't have even attempted using this piece of crap ladder. Couldn't she see it was unsafe?

He choked off saying any of that. "I'll put this junk at the curb and get my ladder for you." He folded the ladder and picked up the broken step. "Glad you weren't hurt."

"I'm fine."

"Be right back."

Completely upended and confused, Jack carted out the ladder. That kiss shouldn't have happened, but it had. Kisses shouldn't turn the world on end, but that one kiss had. A kiss shouldn't have changed everything, but that kiss had.

He met Ray on the front walk, and a spurt of guilt struck. He'd just grabbed Cami and kissed her . . .

"What's with the ladder?" Ray set down the box.

"The step broke, and Cami fell," Jack snarled,

his heart slamming into his throat all over again at the instant replay rush of fear.

Ray straightened sharply. "Is she okay?"

"Yeah, she's fine. I caught her in time. This shit's going to the curb, and I'm bringing over my ladder like I should have."

Jack stomped down the driveway. He should have tossed this old ladder back when he'd helped Wayne sort the house. If he'd been a split second slower, Cami could have been seriously hurt.

He swallowed hard against the potent emotional surge. Oh, hell, that kiss was a mistake. Over the years, he'd wondered what kissing Cami might be like, but he'd never imagined that the reality would be so intense.

You're crazy. Wanting to date Cami is crossing the line, like wanting to date a friend's sister. Yes, Cami's just Ray's sister-in-law, but they're a close-knit family. Are you willing to risk busting up your friendship with Ray and Mikki over Cami?

Right. Logically, acting on that kiss was totally out of the question. Totally unrealistic. Totally crazy.

But she'd kissed him back.

Just happy he'd caught her? No, that was more than a mere thank you kiss. That was a real kiss. There was the hoped-for hint that she might be as interested.

He gritted his teeth. Cami was single and free. He liked and admired so much about her. He finally had a chance to see if there might be something real between them. He'd be a fool if he didn't try.

Don't go off all half-cocked. You need to use your brain. You need a plan.

He grabbed the aluminum stepladder from his

garage and headed next door.

Play it easy, feel things out. That was the best bet. She'd been just as rocked by the kiss as he'd been. He had proximity in his favor now. No need to wait for a party or for a chance encounter.

Convincing Cami they could be so right together might be . . . fascinating. He'd never dated someone he knew so well before. However, if he pulled it off . . .

He grinned. Well, maybe he could have something truly incredible to be thankful for by Thanksgiving. He liked a challenge, right?

Ray hefted the last box from the truck. "Jack, if Cami's finished, Mikki said she and the twins are dying for an ice cream at the boardwalk. Could you see if she wants to join us?"

"Sure."

Back upstairs, he took a steadying breath and stepped into the bedroom. Cami had finished making the bed and stood surveying her job with hands planted on hips and a pleased smile curving her pretty mouth. The queen-sized bed was an inviting expanse of plush comforter and pillows.

The urge to run his hands over the curves her hands rested on, scoop her into his arms, and then discover if another kiss would be just as inspiring was overwhelming. He all too easily pictured them together in that bed, the neatly arranged bedding all disarrayed, and Cami beneath him with her long blond hair strewn over the copper and green pillows.

"Here you go." He leaned the ladder against the wall. "You can hang onto this as long as you need for the painting and all. I don't have any projects going on at home."

"Thanks, I appreciate it."

"That's a heck of a great looking bed."

Her grin sparkled. "I love it. I can't wait to sleep in it. I've always wanted a beautiful bed, and I decided, since I was moving, why not now? The time had come to stop holding off for that nebulous 'someday when I get married.' Of course, the room still needs work."

She swept her hand around the room. The tired blue paint of the walls needed changing, and the ceiling fan was functional, but ugly. "Once it's repainted and my new curtains are up, it should be lovely in here."

"I like the colors of the comforter and pillows."

"I wanted something warm and rich to snuggle in on a cold winter night. I'm always chilly in the winter." She laughed lightly.

He'd be more than happy to keep her warm.

Jack clenched the doorframe, his jeans again abruptly uncomfortable. He cleared his throat. "I meant to tell you earlier, I finished Emily's bed. Also, Ray says Mikki wants some ice cream at the boardwalk. Are you interested?"

"Sure. Ice cream sounds good. Are you going to join us?"

Feeling like a moth to a flame, he grinned. "Absolutely."

~*~

Cami woke the next morning with the memory of Jack's mouth on hers sharp and clear. That kiss had prominently repeated itself throughout her dreams last night. That kiss was just a thing of the moment, brought on by adrenaline. He was dating

Angela. He'd apologized. She needed to put it behind her, focus on moving day, and keep an eye on Mikki.

Groaning, she rolled out of her bed on the couch and headed for the bathroom. Mom and Dad would be arriving any minute, bright and early.

At least she wouldn't be seeing Jack until four at the earliest. Ray had told him not to waste a personal day and to just come by after school, so she had hours to settle herself about that kiss before she had to face him.

Only, when she pulled up to the curb, Jack emerged from his garage, dressed in shorts, tank top, and work boots.

He waved. "Good morning."

"I thought you weren't coming by until after school."

"I decided to take the day anyhow." He grinned. "What's the use of personal days if you don't bother taking one now and then? I've helped enough people move to learn that moving is always twice as hard as you think it will be. Moving a couple blocks is just as hard and time consuming as moving to another state. So I'm here."

"Well, thank you for the help."

"What are you tackling first?"

"Mikki's feeling anxious and asked if I would paint the nursery for them instead of helping with the moving."

"All the better that I took the day off then. She's feeling okay?"

"Just ordinary nesting anxiety and frustration at being unable to do everything herself. Physically, she and the babies are doing totally great."

"Good. I'll unload your stuff from the garage until Ray, Kerr, Brian, and Hale get here, and then we'll coordinate from there. I saw all your boxes and things are marked with rooms, so that makes it easy. If anything's put in the wrong place, I'll shift it for you later."

"Thank you. Sounds good."

Painting the nursery kept a safe space between them for the morning, but his passing by in the hall with furniture and boxes only piqued her heightened awareness of his presence.

Painting the nursery also emphasized her own persistent single state. Always the auntie . . .

She sighed. No matter last evening's surprising kiss, at the rate she was going with men, she'd never be setting up her own nursery. Brent had proved to like only the idea of a family, not actually getting around to starting one. Why did she keep finding man after man who didn't stand by his word? She swallowed against the sharp ache. Why couldn't she find her own Ray? Maybe she needed Mikki's list after all.

Two knocks came at the door.

She straightened from her crouch to find Jack leaning casually in the doorway, muscular shoulders and arms shown off by the sweaty gray tank top. She brushed her bangs away with the back of her hand. This late toasty burst of Indian summer and breezeless day made painting hot work. Jack standing there looking so tasty wasn't helping the heat.

He glanced around the nursery. "Hey, there. How goes the painting? Nice color. I was expecting a lot more pink."

"The ceiling and one wall coat are almost done. One to go. The pink will arrive in the accessories."

The ivory blush walls would work perfectly with the antique look Mikki envisioned for the room.

"I checked in on Mikki. She's having fun with your mom setting up the kitchen. Emily's helping." He chuckled and rolled his eyes. "Want some help in here?"

"No, I'm good. I'm sure Ray and the others need you more with unloading the house and the truck."

"Okay, if you're sure."

She waved her paint roller. "Perfectly fine."

"See you later then."

She turned back to the wall and sighed. She really should have accepted his help. She could do this, but two extra hands would have been handy.

With the second coat finished, she headed downstairs for a lunch break, more water, and a check in on Mikki and Mom.

Mom hugged her. "Hey, sweetie. How's it going upstairs?"

"Slow, but making progress."

"Okay, my lovely ladies, here's more kitchen boxes. Where do you want them? Oh, great! Food's here. I'm starving." Ray lugged a small heavy box, followed by Dad, Jack, Kerr Driscoll, Brian Fielding, and Hale Lindstrom, also laden with boxes.

Mikki looked around the kitchen that looked like packing materials had exploded, the mess not helped by the fort Emily built out of the kitchen table, boxes, and packing papers. The only neat area was the island covered with sandwiches, salads, and other food from the deli. "Oh, stack them along the wall for now. Lunch is all set. Just grab what you want."

Cami pulled a water bottle from the fridge. "Anyone want a cold drink while I have the fridge open? Dad, iced tea for you?"

"Thanks, Cami."

"I'll take an iced tea, too. Thanks." Ray patted Emily, who'd peeked out from her table fort. "Nice fort, kiddo."

Kerr snagged a dill pickle. "Bottle of water for me."

"Make that two waters." Hale waded through crumpled papers to wash up at the sink.

"Three waters," said Brian.

"Grab me an iced tea while you're there, Cami, please. Thanks." Jack scrubbed his tank over his face, baring nicely taut abs.

She wrenched her attention back to handing out drinks.

Jack tipped his head back for a long swallow of tea.

No, thinking how sexy he looked swallowing the cold drink was not helping matters.

"That hit the spot. How's the nursery going?"

"Both coats are done. I'll tackle the trim next and then the changing table."

Mom handed Emily a cookie. "Mikki, I told you to keep the old one. I don't know why you didn't just buy one with the new cribs. That one you have looks like you found it at the curb."

Cami choked down a giggle and exchanged a smile with Mikki. Actually, Mikki had, pulling the minivan over to the curb like a crazy woman, practically tires screeching to a halt, and begged

Cami to wrestle the thing into the back.

"I know, I know. However, at the time, Laura needed a crib and changing table, and we desperately needed the space. Once it's painted and has the new pad on top, it will look perfect." Mikki propped her feet up on a box and rubbed a hand over her heavy belly. "Jack, why don't you give Cami a hand with the painting. Please? I feel so bad she's doing all the work."

Jack grinned. "No problem, I'd be glad to help. Ray? You good?"

"Yeah. Go on with Cami. My parents are keeping things organized at the cottage, and between Kerr, Hale, Brian, and me, we have enough hands for loading and unloading the truck. I'm with Mikki. I'd like that room finished in case the girls decide to make an early appearance."

Cami groaned inwardly but smiled. "Okay, thanks."

Ray's parents arrived, and everyone loaded their plates with food and headed out to the deck to eat and enjoy the sunshine.

Jack sat across from her. "So how's the school year going for you? The little munchkins settling down?"

Cami smiled. Some people thought she was nuts for loving to teach first grade, but she was happy to leave all the teen angst, rebellion, and drama of the upper grades to teachers like Jack who relished the challenges that came with his high school students. The little ones were always so eager to learn, so enthusiastic about everything in their lives, as if every day was a big adventure.

"They're getting into the routine finally. An

active bunch this year, talkative is an understatement, but they love stories and, amazingly, pretty much sit good as gold at story time. How goes your crew?"

He grimaced. "We will survive. However, each year just reminds me once again how thankful I am to no longer be a teen."

Painting the trim and all the narrow bits of the window grills was much easier with Jack's help and she had to admit they worked well together. She also had to admit to enjoying his company. They'd been good friends for six years. One accidental kiss couldn't change that connection.

Soon they had the last strip of molding painted, the changing table coated, new ceiling fixture installed, and the painting equipment tidied and out of the room.

"Pizza and beer's here!" Ray shouted up the stairs. "We're serving up on the deck. Come and get it!"

"Terrific, I'm starved." Jack scanned the nursery with a satisfied grin. "Done. Looking good in here, if I may say so myself."

Once decorated, the nursery was going to be adorable. "All that's left to do is move in the furniture and hang the curtains and decorations. Then Mikki can fill all the drawers and the closet with the gifts from the shower."

The food was laid out and ready. Tired but happy, Cami filled her plate with salad and a huge slice of pepperoni pizza and grabbed a beer.

Mikki raised her cup. "I can't believe how great the place looks already. Thank you, everyone. You all are just the best!"

Ray kissed her forehead. "The weather forecast

looks good for Sunday. I think we need to inaugurate the place with a barbeque and have some people over. What do you say, honey?"

"Sounds good to me."

"Jack, you'll come, right? Bring Angela, too." Mikki added. "We haven't seen her in a while."

"No, Angela and I broke up." Jack shrugged and took a big bite of pizza.

Cami inhaled her sip of beer. At least her coughing covered up her shock.

Mikki patted her back. "Oh, Jack, I'm so sorry. She was nice."

"No big deal. Yeah, Angela's real nice, but it was one of those summer relationships that was just fun. She and I agreed we weren't really going anywhere solid and were better off as friends. Different life goals, you know?"

Jack was unattached. Cami shivered. They were *both* unattached, at the same time.

Her crush emitted an enthusiastic squeak. That kiss was no longer a mistake but an intriguing bit of temptation.

~*~

Sunday arrived, the impromptu potluck housewarming party was in full swing, and Jack had yet to figure out his next move. He struggled to be cool, but his mind kept chewing over that kiss, that bed, and that moment of fear before he stopped her fall. He kept looking for a good moment to talk to Cami, but the lively party kept her busy with Mikki, and he kept changing his mind on how to open the subject.

This hesitant second-guessing wasn't like him at all. He had a case of lovelorn pining as bad as any of his angsty teen students. Worse, because when he'd been in high school, he would have just gone for the prize. Even then, he'd had the asking out on a date routine honed smooth and easy, and he'd never stressed much over the possibility of being shot down.

Except Cami meant something, and that changed everything.

Although everyone was beat after two days of moving and getting things settled, the party was a welcome break and great fun. Cami and Mikki's parents came, along with an assortment of friends and neighbors, and small kids ran underfoot inside and out. Mikki was in high spirits and didn't argue when folks fussed over her.

After cleaning up from dessert, some folks headed home and the rest settled into the living room with drinks and coffee to watch the baseball game.

Mikki waddled from the kitchen, one hand planted on the small of her back. "Jack, have you seen Cami?"

Cami had been in the kitchen. "Maybe she ran next door for a minute? Do you need her?"

"No, I'm fine. Heading for the sofa. I was just wondering where she was."

Jack found Cami sitting out on the deck steps.

"Hey, there you are. Mikki was looking for you."

"Is she okay? Does she need me?"

"No. All's well. She was just wondering where you were." He sat beside her on the step.

"I came out to watch the sunset and lost track of time. The colors are gorgeous. It's such a beautiful evening."

The last of sunset light cast a vibrant golden glow, and the warm evening felt more like summer than October, even with the autumn yellows and oranges tinting the trees and fallen leaves scattered over the lawn.

She flashed him a wry smile. "To be honest, I was indulging in a moment of self-pity. Feeling sorry for myself being the single one in that crowd of happy couples and families."

"Yeah, I know what you mean."

"Most of the time, I'm okay with it, but sometimes it gets to me. Particularly when they're all going on about their kids."

Hell, how he knew that feeling.

"Don't you just love the questions? All the polite variations on why aren't you married yet? Like I can make that happen all on my own." He clamped his mouth shut, not meaning to have blurted that bitterness.

"Exactly." She sipped at her drink. "I wanted to say I'm sorry about you and Angela. Why didn't you mention anything?"

Jack shrugged. There really was nothing much to say. "We had a great time together, but it was over. I didn't really think about it. As break-ups go, it was a painless one. We're still friends." A sad statement, really, that their relationship hadn't mattered enough for the break-up to hurt.

Cami nodded. "We were both lucky, I guess. Brent was nice and all, but he . . ." Her eyes filled with the pain that she rarely let anyone see and she turned her face away. No matter her calm words, her break-up had hurt.

"Just wasn't the one." He hated seeing her

hurting. That was another big concern with Cami—she could be the *one*. With Cami, the consequences of a break-up would be complicated and definitely painful.

"Right." She stirred her ice around. "Anyhow, it's probably for the best. Things are going to be busy and crazy around here for a while. Getting settled, decorating, helping Mikki get ready for the babies, then all of a sudden the babies will be here, it'll be the end of the first marking period, time for report cards, parent conferences, and Gerry and his family will be here for Thanksgiving, and then, bam, it's all the school and church holiday activities racing into Christmas and New Year's Eve. No time for dating in all that anyhow. Instead of wanting to go out, I'll more likely be begging to crawl home for a hot bath, glass of wine, and a nap."

Yes, picturing Cami relaxing in a bathtub of bubbles or curled up napping on that new bed of hers came all too easily. He chuckled. "I don't think I've seen Ray happier or more of a nervous wreck."

Cami sighed and sipped at her drink. "I'm so happy for them. This has been a totally different experience from when they were expecting Emily, hasn't it? Mikki's doing awesomely, but I know I've reached the jump every time the phone rings stage."

"I know what you mean."

"I originally thought their buying the house and trying to move now of all times was on the crazy side, but really, the whole project has been good for Mikki, keeping her occupied with planning and decorating. She hates being off her feet so much."

"So, what are your plans for the apartment? Paint? Wallpaper? Any remodeling?"

"No remodeling. The kitchen's dated but in decent shape, so no need to change anything there more than freshening up with paint and wallpaper. Although, I might change out the faucets and the cabinet door pulls. I really need more hours in the day."

Would she be game for him to help her? That might be a way to feel his way into asking her out on a real date.

A cool breeze filtered into the unusually mild evening. A yellow leaf fluttered to the lawn, then another.

Cami rolled her shoulders and winced.

"You okay?"

"Yes. I'm just a little stiff from the painting. I don't normally try to paint a whole room top to bottom in one day, and I'm paying for it. Thanks for helping me finish."

Before he really considered his action, he'd set aside his drink and was massaging her shoulders.

After her surprised start under his hands, she sighed, a sweet needy groan that drove a twist of desire through his gut. Maybe touching her was a mistake, but he stayed put, gently working his thumbs into her tense muscles.

"Oh, that feels so good. Thank you." She flexed into his hands like a kitten for a petting, complete bliss on her face.

He swallowed against the constricting knot in his throat. "Any time."

Oh, yes, this massage was a tactical error. Visions of following the path of his hands with kisses tempted, but he continued his slow massage, reaching her nape and working up her neck to the base of her skull, satisfying himself with the pleasure of feeling her relax.

He dropped his hands away. "There you go."

She rolled her shoulders and gave him a brilliant smile. "Oh, so much better. Thank you."

Oh, yeah, he was in deep.

A squadron of geese honked noisily northward, dark silhouettes against the dull rose and purples of the fading sunset.

Cami laughed and pushed to her feet. "Silly things are heading the wrong direction. Maybe just getting their bearings. Let's head inside and see if there's any coffee left."

Chapter Three

ONE OF CAMI'S FAVORITE BONUSES OF THE NEW place was sharing a cup of tea with Mikki before heading off to work, a habit they'd begun in September at the cottage.

"Have anyone you'd like to bring to the Halloween party?" Mikki rubbed her belly. Poor Mikki was growing more and more uncomfortable every day. "If we have the party, of course."

"No." The man she was interested in would already be there. Could she ask about Jack? She sipped at her tea. "I've been thinking . . . Maybe you're right. I think I've been meeting the wrong kind of men."

There, she'd admitted there might be a pattern in her dating life of choosing men who didn't put their all into a relationship.

"I need to change that."

Mikki slipped her hand around Cami's and gave a reassuring squeeze. "You'll find the right man for you."

"I thought I was finding good men."

"You were. They were good men, just . . . incredibly boring." Mikki winced. "Sorry, but they were. All very pleasant, kind, hardworking, and totally flat-line on the zing scale. And none of them put you first in their lives.

She hated how right Mikki was. She'd settled for a warm buzz, she'd settled for comfortable instead of right, safe instead of passionate. Her parents had passion. Ray and Mikki had passion.

"I want you to find someone like Ray. He might seem ordinary on the outside, and yes, he's nice, pleasant, and kind, but for me, he's a ten on the zing scale. He didn't hide that he was interested in me. He didn't give up when his job went crazy, and he didn't give up when Daddy did his papa bear 'You're not good enough for my princess' routine. He treats me like Daddy treats Mom, like I'm his everything. Well, saying that sounds sort of obsessive, but in a sexy, loving, wholesome way."

"I get what you mean, but I never knew Daddy tried to scare off Ray."

"I didn't know at the time. Ray told me the whole story later. He was all puffed up about it. He actually liked that Daddy gave him a real hard time. Men are so weird. I just know Ray will want to pull that stunt with our girls."

Cami frowned. "Daddy never did that to any of my boyfriends. He always acted as if he liked them. I thought I was doing the right thing."

"Because none of your guys were a real threat to

take his little girl away. All nice, but very meh."

"So I've been going about dating all wrong? Maybe I should look for a man like Jack. He's not boring." She bit her lip.

Mikki winced like she'd tasted something unpleasant. "Ahh . . ."

"What? Jack is Ray's best friend. What's wrong with Jack?"

"Nothing. I adore Jack. He's like a brother to me, but really, he's never shown the slightest inclination to settle down. You know, the moment a relationship looks like it could get serious, he's always off to a new girl. I had hopes with Angela, but, no, again he dropped her before it could get serious."

"So he sleeps around."

"No, no, no, I didn't say that or mean that. I simply mean you should look for a guy who isn't boring *and* wants to have a permanent relationship. Oh, I don't know what I'm saying. Just Brent was too utterly boring and beneath you, and a guy like Jack is, well, just too . . . Jack. I can't see you being happy with a guy like Jack long-term, that's all. I don't want your heart broken. I know Ray would agree. Someone in between the two, maybe? Somebody just right."

"So I'm Goldilocks?"

Mikki spilled into laughter. "No! Oh—forget most of what I said and just be open to the guy who has some zing."

Monday at school began like so many Mondays, completely busy with chatter and interruptions, and made even more hectic by all the catch-up work and her students fascinated by her two-day absence.

When she sent them off to lunch and hid in her classroom to work, even having to grade math tests was a complete relief in the blessed silence.

"So, all settled in the new place?" Cami's best friend and fellow teacher Pat perched on the corner of Cami's desk.

Cami leaned back in her chair. "Not even close. Moving is such a bear."

"And you've basically moved twice in two months."

"One and a half times, since I never unpacked at my sister's. But I'm all done living out of a suitcase."

"Which is why I brought you this." Pat set a heavy, glittery gift bag on Cami's desk. The top of a wine bottle peeped out amid the tissue paper fluff.

"Aw, thanks." Cami pulled out a bottle of Pouilly-Fuissé, a loaf of crusty bread, olive oil, sea salt, and a bag of chocolate truffles. "Oh, these are so great. I love this wine. Thanks!" She hugged Pat.

"I thought they'd help you and Brent enjoy celebrating your new place."

Cami sighed. Life had been so busy, she had forgotten to tell Pat the now old news. "Brent is no longer in the picture."

"Oh, no, I'm sorry."

She filled Pat in on end of the fizzled relationship.

"I'm sorry he was such an ass at the end, but I'm glad you're okay. Any new men on the horizon?" Pat raised a perfectly penciled brow.

Cami hesitated too long before her reply. "No."

"That sounded far from a concrete no. There's someone you'd like to have on the horizon?"

"No. Maybe. I'm not sure. I'm sure he wouldn't

be a good idea."

"Ooh, there is one? Tell me every last detail."

"Mikki and Ray cannot hear a word about this."

"My lips are sealed."

"I really don't know how to handle what happened on Thursday. You've met Ray's friend Jack?"

"Yummy hot teacher with the gorgeous blue eyes? How could I forget him?"

"Well . . . he kissed me."

"A kiss or a *kiss*?"

Cami groaned. "The forget where you are and why kissing him is a bad idea kind of kiss."

"Awesome. You go girl!"

"I just don't know what to do."

"Seems simple to me. He's interested in you. You're interested in him. Let nature take its course."

"We're friends and neighbors. Until Thursday, he'd never even let off a hint he's interested."

"Sounds to me like he's interested now. "

"But he's a friend."

"Friends is a good place to start a relationship."

"So much could go wrong. He's a neighbor now, and more, he's Ray's best friend. What if I try this, it goes wrong, and we break up? It's not just us involved, but Ray and Mikki and even Emily and the babies and where I live . . ."

"Cami, honey, stop focusing on all the things that could go wrong and think of all the things that could go right. What if Jack is the one for you? What if you miss out on the love of your life because you were afraid to take a risk? Tell me, if he wasn't a neighbor and Ray's friend, would you be interested? Be honest now."

Cami slumped in her seat with a long groan and covered both eyes with her hands. "Yes!"

"So you know what you have to do. Give the guy a chance. What are the positive things about Jack?"

"He's smart and interesting to talk with. Loves teaching and is good with kids. He's handy with tools. He's a good friend. He makes me laugh. Somehow we always end up hanging together at Mikki and Ray's parties."

That particular realization was a surprise. They always did hang out together, even when they'd brought dates.

"Oh, he can cook."

"That's a plus. Hotly handsome isn't hurting here either."

"True." She grinned.

"And downsides? He's a man, so there has to be some. He leaves the toilet seat up? Slob?"

Cami laughed. Coming up with negatives was difficult. Jack was a good guy and far more positive traits than bad filled her head. "He keeps his house tidy, at least when I've seen it, but he does seem to thoroughly enjoy his bachelor life and have a girl of the month habit. He hasn't shown any inclination to settle down. And he's very into his sports activities. Although he's great with Emily, I don't actually know if he wants kids of his own someday."

However, honest sadness had filled his voice last night while he commiserated with her over their single state in the midst of couples. Was he as into being single as she'd always assumed?

"As for wanting kids, why not just ask him? Or have Mikki ask him."

"And have Mikki ask why I want to know? She already thinks Jack is the wrong kind of guy for me."

"You are the only one who can decide if a guy is the right one for you. You and Mikki may be twins, but you are completely different people. Be honest with yourself. What do you want for you?"

"Mikki said I need someone with zing."

"She's right about that. Anyone could tell Brent was totally without zing. So, for you, Jack has zing?"

Cami covered her face with her hands, blushing madly. "Oh, yes."

"Then you have two choices: play it safe and live with regrets, or go for the gusto and see if he's the one."

"You're right."

"Of course I am. I'm your best friend." Pat's chuckles burst into rollicking laughter, and Cami was suddenly laughing along with her.

They caught their breath.

"I just don't want to make a mistake. Mikki seemed so adamant that a guy like Jack would be a mistake."

"Then don't say anything to Mikki until you're more certain. You can give the guy a chance and still be careful, you know. If Jack's as good a friend as he sounds, he won't be careless with you either. Be smart, but be open to possibility."

"Okay."

"And I want to know every last detail."

"Pat!"

Pat grinned wickedly. "Hey, I need all the romance I can get in my life."

~*~

Jack stopped by Ray and Mikki's each evening to lend a hand in getting them settled, and he made sure to help Cami with at least one small thing in her place each day as well.

Biding his time to ask her out was hard. Holding off stealing another kiss to test if last week's world-rocking kiss was more than a fluke was harder, but his gut warned for patience. Simply spending time with Cami crystalized his determination to win her for his own.

On Friday night, he arrived home from the gym just as Mikki and Ray pulled into the driveway.

Ray rolled down the window. "Hey, are you up for being lazy with some pizza and a movie? We're just back from the doctor's and shopping, and we're both too tired to work on the house tonight."

"Sure."

"Come on over when you're ready then."

After Jack washed up and changed, he headed over with a bottle of Cami's favorite merlot.

He knocked at Ray and Mikki's door and walked in. "Hey, everybody. How was your day?"

"TGIF for me." Cami waved from the kitchen.

The intense leap of delight at seeing Cami sharpened his frustration, and he wanted to believe her smile was for him, not just because it was Friday evening. He raised the wine bottle. "TGIF indeed. Glass of wine, Cami and Ray?"

"I'd love a glass, thanks."

"Pour one for me, too." Ray handed off a glass of iced tea to Mikki. "The checkup went real good today. The ultrasound was amazing. It looked like Kaylie was sucking her thumb. The cutest thing you ever saw. We have the pic on my tablet. You two have got to see it. The doctor said Mikki and the babies are doing super, but he wants Mikki to take things real easy now and stay off her feet as much as possible."

"My feet want me off them, too, and I think it was Christie who was sucking her thumb." Mikki smiled at Emily, who was dancing in and out of the kitchen, tossing her curls, and singing some nonsense song.

Would he be as enthusiastic as Ray at the prospect of twins? He wanted a family someday, but seeing Mikki in discomfort like this and two at once? With the history of twins running in their family, he had to consider the possibility if he and Cami became a couple.

He glanced at Cami, and the warm sinking sensation in his chest was all acceptance. Yeah, he could tackle anything for Cami.

They all settled into the living room for the pizza and movie.

With Mikki on the sofa and Ray in the recliner beside her, that left the cushy love seat for Cami and Jack.

If only he had the freedom to tug her close. "So, what are your plans for the weekend?"

"I'm painting my bedroom tomorrow. As much as I'd like to relax, I really can't finish unpacking or get settled until I have all the painting done."

"I don't have plans. Why don't I give you a hand?" Jack offered as casually as possible.

"The weather's supposed to be perfect tomorrow. I'm sure you have better things to do than waste your day painting. You're running out of good weather to go kayaking."

"I honestly want to help."

"I can do it."

"Go on, Cami. Take Jack up on his offer. We've been totally monopolizing you all week. Now that we're mostly unpacked, it's your turn to get settled. I just wish I could help more." Mikki stroke her bulging belly. "Well, at all."

"I've enjoyed helping you, you know that."

"And we've appreciated it."

Time to refocus the conversation on his goal. "I really want to help. Just because you can do it by yourself, doesn't mean you have to."

"Okay, okay. I accept. Thank you."

Yes! He settled back, jazzed to have made another step forward.

He was still jazzed in the morning when he headed next door, even as he reminded himself to take things easy. This was not a date. This was simply spending time together to feel things out. This was just the same as all the other times they'd spent the day together at the beach, hiking, or kayaking—except, this time they'd be alone.

Cami opened her front door and a hefty punch of desire stopped his greeting in his throat. Her face was flushed, looking fresh-scrubbed, and she wore an old T-shirt and paint-smudged jeans, with her hair pulled back into a ponytail.

"Hi, Jack. Ready for a day of painting?"

"Looking forward to it."

"Why you'd want to be inside on such a beautiful day when you could be kayaking or hiking, I don't know, but come on in."

He stepped into her living room, greeted by the scents of fresh coffee, baked bread, and cinnamon.

"Smells awesome in here."

"I was feeling domestic this morning and made cinnamon rolls. They're just out of the oven. Want some coffee and a roll?

"Sure. I never pass up your baking." She always baked from scratch, and everything she cooked was delicious.

While they ate, they discussed her plans for the apartment. She wanted to begin with the bedroom and finish with the living room. Previous tenants had been given an unfortunate free rein with the paint colors throughout the apartment, and most of the walls were deep wild tones and marred with nail holes. They had some spackling work and a coat or two of primer ahead before painting with the warm, light colors Cami had chosen.

"I would have emptied the closet and taken down the outlet covers and curtain rods, but making the rolls distracted me."

"Those are easy, and the rolls are great." He caved to temptation and snagged a second roll off the serving plate.

While Cami emptied the closet and covered the bed and floor with drop cloths, Jack dropped the ceiling fan and removed the curtain rods and painted-over outlet covers. Next, she worked on patching the walls while he cut in the primer around the ceiling. At least the previous tenants had left the ceiling white.

The priming proceeded smoothly, and they also added in the hallway to the job, alternating between the two spaces as they waited for each coat to dry before the next.

Noon came, and they took a lunch break down

in the kitchen.

Jack knew what he wanted to say. He had her full attention. They had privacy.

Sucking in a deep breath, he met her eyes. "Hey, Cami, I was wondering if—"

Three firm raps knocked at the kitchen breezeway door, followed by Mikki's cheerful "Hello!"

Cami turned away. "Come on in."

Aw, damn. That was a close call. He jammed his hopes into stand-by and picked up the two plates.

~*~

Cami hadn't fully considered the impact of working alone with Jack all day in the close confines of her bedroom.

Even after a week, that kiss remained fresh and vibrant in her mind. As they worked, she rode on a crazy seesaw from relieved he was being a perfect friend and gentleman to totally frustrated he hadn't tried to kiss her again so she could explore the potential promised in that kiss.

Jack appeared totally opposite the sort of man she thought she wanted. Only, when she broke down his traits, so many met her own "list."

Stable career – Yes.

Financially Responsible – Yes.

Good with kids – Yes.

Friendly – Yes.

Intelligent – Yes.

Good relationship with family and friends –Yes.

Sense of humor – Yes.

Easy to talk to – Yes.

Shared similar interests – Yes.

However, she also wanted a man who was into

permanence and wanted a family, and that remained an unknown quantity with Jack. He tended to pick women with sports or social activities in mind and certainly hadn't shown a desire for permanence with them, and the girlfriends with whom she'd had any conversations of note had chatted enthusiastically about their busy, childfree career plans.

However, he owned a house with plenty of room for that family she'd never asked if he wanted. Unlike Kerr and Brian, who bought, rehabbed, and sold house after house, Jack seemed content to keep the big four-bedroom ranch he'd bought as a handyman special for the rest of his life. Odd for a single man to have all that space he never used.

Jack tapped down the lid on the paint tin. "How about we call it a day? I'm starving."

"You're always starving."

He grinned. "True. Come on, let's clean up, and I'll treat you to supper."

"Oh, you don't have to do that. I can put something together here."

"I was thinking of finding something greasy, salty, and totally unhealthy at the boardwalk and then follow up with ice cream or an Italian ice and a long sunset walk. It's a beautiful day, and we've been stuck indoors all day. What do you say?"

He gave that irresistible smile of his, and warmth filled her heart.

"Okay."

They had worked hard and deserved a fun break. She always enjoyed a walk on the boardwalk, playing at the arcades, and people-watching, and the aquarium had been a big hit with Emily over the summer. She had no excuses or obligations to keep her from saying yes. Ray and Mikki had left two hours ago for a party at his boss's house, and Emily was spending the night with Ray's parents.

He tugged her paintbrush from her grip. "Great, wash your hands and grab your jacket. I'll wrap this for you."

Despite a cool breeze off the ocean, it was a Saturday, and the wide boardwalk was busy with people of all ages out to enjoy a walk or a jog, a meal, meet friends at the bar, or play the arcade games. Down on the mostly empty beach, a few kids ran and played, and several beachcombers searched the waterline for shells and sea glass.

Jack chose the Italian hot dog slathered in peppers, Cami decided on half a sausage, peppers, and onion sub, both ordered lemonade, and as a compromise toward healthy eating, they shared one large order of curly fries.

They found an empty bench facing the beach and settled down to eat their messy, tasty meal. When they ran out of napkins, Cami fished the package of wipes from her purse.

Jack accepted the offered wipe with a grin. "Sure sign of an elementary school teacher."

Cami laughed. "And an aunt of a three-year-old. Have to be prepared. I also have tissues, princess bandages, and strawberry-scented hand sanitizer."

After Italian ices for dessert and playing for a short time in an arcade and winning a plush Teddy bear for Emily, they strolled the boardwalk, enjoying the last light of sunset. When they reached the north end, they stopped and stood looking out to the Manasquan Inlet and dark ocean cloaked in twilight.

"Hey, Cami?" Jack touched a hand to her shoulder.

She turned and met his eyes. The deep emotion in his face went far beyond simple friendship, far beyond the companionable rapport of the past day. Questions simmered in that look. He meant to kiss her. She froze, torn between yes and no.

He skimmed his hand along her shoulder and up to cradle her head, giving her all the time in the world to step away.

She didn't.

He lowered his mouth to hers. The kiss was slow, sweet, and simple, a caress of lips, yet, somehow, this gentle kiss was more potent and dizzying than his impulsive, searing kiss after her fall from the ladder.

This time he didn't say sorry.

This time she didn't say they shouldn't have.

He quirked a smile as he stepped away and wrapped her hand in his, and they resumed their walk.

Jack was quiet on the short drive home until he turned onto their street. "So, more painting tomorrow? Still want some help?"

She paused before answering, pondering that kiss and his patient, hopeful smile. If he were around, no doubt another kiss would happen. Two kisses already held enough combustible chemistry that another was inevitable. Was she really ready to take the risks and see if they had a future beyond friends?

So, decide. Risk or regret. Yes or no?

She was afraid of the risks, but so very tired of regrets. "Yes, thanks. I want to finish the bedroom and tackle the kitchen. I'd appreciate the help."

"Then I'll see you tomorrow." He parked in his driveway and walked her to her door.

"Thanks for the help today and thanks for supper. I had fun."

Dying from the suspense as she opened the door, Cami brushed a quick goodnight kiss to his mouth and stepped back before either of them could turn the kiss serious. "See you in the morning."

Jack just nodded with an easy smile, as if he knew her turmoil, and turned to walk down her steps.

She slipped inside and let out a heavy exhale, head swimming with all the ways that this thing with Jack could go wrong.

Stop borrowing trouble. Stop panicking over two kisses. Well, three kisses now. Focus on what could go right.

Right, and those had been wonderful kisses . . .

Chapter Four

IF EVER A KISS WAS A POSITIVE ANSWER, THEIR KISS on the boardwalk had been. Jack had never been happier to stroll home alone after a rushed kiss and shut door. His plan was working. Now to get over dodging the question.

The next morning he woke to a dark, blustery, rainy day, filled with a chill autumn snap, but not even the gloomy weather could dampen his anticipation as he dashed next door through the downpour.

Today, Cami wanted to work on her kitchen. She'd picked a calm white and green fern print wallpaper to brighten up the room from its current dark blue paint and maroon country print wallpaper border.

Jack studied the kitchen's awkward layout. When he'd gutted his kitchen four years ago, Cami had given him helpful input on how someone who baked and cooked as much as she did liked a kitchen arranged. This space was not a cook's kitchen. The sink here was tucked at an angle in the corner, there wasn't enough workspace, and the countertop of gold-flecked faux-marble laminate might have looked sharp once, but the surface was scratched and stained.

"You could use more counter space. We could move the cabinets around and get the sink centered under the window for you. If I wrangled Kerr and Hale into helping, the job would take hardly any time."

"True, and thanks for the offer, but this is a hundred times better than my old apartment's little kitchen and I don't need the mess right now. I'd love a better countertop, and maybe down the road we'll change it out, but for now, I'll hit it with bleach, a little elbow grease, and some laminate polish."

"Are you planning to paint the cabinets?"

"No, they're in okay shape, and I like the old pine look, so I think a good scrubbing and polishing should do the trick."

After pouring coffees, they got to work. The old border came down easily, and they set to scrubbing, patching, and priming the kitchen walls and painting the ceiling.

Jack focused on the work, chatting with Cami, and keeping his hands to himself, all while pondering how best to ask her out. A straightforward enough task, but he didn't want to fumble his chances either. However, each time he thought he had a plan settled, he hesitated.

While they waited for the primer and paint to

dry, Cami made them lunch.

She pinned him with a puzzled look. "Jack, is everything okay? You've been very quiet this morning."

Okay, so he wasn't being as cool and easy as he supposed. "No, I'm fine. Just had some stuff running through my mind."

"If you had something else you needed to be doing, I can finish this on my own."

"No, I'm good." Well, aside from acting worse than a kid mooning around and trying to work up the courage to ask the unobtainable girl to the prom.

A knock came at the breezeway door.

"Come on in," Cami called out.

Ray poked his head in. "Hey, looking good in here. Mikki wants to know if you two want chicken or steaks tonight."

"I'm good either way. I'll make her favorite green beans."

"Both sound good to me." Jack nodded at the refrigerator where he'd stashed an apple pie. "I brought dessert."

"Thanks. See you in a little."

The downside to papering the small kitchen was all the tedious odd lengths and shapes to measure and cut.

The bigger downside was that focusing on the detailed work took his attention off finding the best moment to ask her out. Yes, he was definitely overthinking things, but he also had to concede a hefty portion of avoidance factored in. If he didn't ask, then she couldn't say no.

They finished the last bit just in time to clean up and head next door for supper and the National

League Division series game.

Good friends, good food, good times. He always felt so at home with Ray, Mikki, and Cami, as if they were family, rather than simply his closest friends.

"We need to make a decision." Ray announced over supper. "Do we still want to have our annual Halloween-World Series party here on the thirty-first as we originally planned? It's getting close, and we need to let folks know one way or the other."

"I think we should." Mikki sipped at her water. "I really want to have a party. I'm feeling good. Yes, I know, anything could happen in the next three weeks and the babies could be here any day at this point, but I'd hate to cancel. What if we turn the party into an open house potluck and just warn everyone to stay flexible if the twins decide to make an early appearance? Please, hon? What do you think?"

"If you're sure?"

"I'll help, of course," Cami offered.

"And I will, too." Jack gave Mikki a thumbs-up. She loved her Halloween parties, and he'd be glad to help.

Cami fetched a notepad and the guest list, and they drafted the new party plan and shopping list.

"We could ask Katie if she'd like to bring one of her pies. Ooh! Nadine could bring her seven-layer dip." Mikki licked her lips. "I'll tell her the girls want it."

"No jalapeno peppers for you," Cami warned.

"I know, I know, they upset my insides, but they taste sooo good."

"Jack, are your parents still coming? Do you think your mom would mind bringing a dessert?"

"She'd love to bring one, I'm sure. The last I talked to them about the party, they're coming down that morning and will stay over at my place, since Dad doesn't like to drive late at night anymore."

After more discussion, Cami and Mikki wrote up the email with the revised party plans. Cami would make a pot of chili and an apple pie, Jack volunteered to make his ribs, and Mikki and Ray would make cookies with Emily.

With that chore done, they settled down to eating apple pie and watching the baseball game. The urge to pull Cami to him and snuggle remained a constant nagging annoyance through all nine innings, but he kept a safe arm's length away in the recliner.

After a great game, Cami and Jack were both yawning as they walked through the breezeway into her place to collect his jacket from her living room.

"Thank you for all your help today. I had fun and the kitchen looks so good." Cami brushed a kiss to his lips and lingered, steadying herself with a hand to his waist.

"You're welcome."

He slid his hands around her waist, enjoying how she sighed and softened into his embrace and the lazy exploring kiss. Her hands skimmed to his shoulders, bringing them close, body to body. If she were unready for a new relationship, would she be this comfortable in their kiss, no less steamy for all the gentle nibbles and relaxed caresses?

He leaned back against the living room wall, settling her against him and grazing his hands down to rest on the soft curves of her hips. They sank into the kiss, riding together slow and easy as his body hardened, and his imagination raced at how good they would feel together, skin to skin. If only . . .

However, not tonight. He wasn't rushing any of this. With Cami, patience was simple; just being in the moment was perfect.

At the end of the rich, timeless kiss, Cami tipped her head back, meeting his eyes, her own eyes dark and contemplative.

He gave her a smile. If only he could read those spinning thoughts of hers. "That was nice."

She nodded and sipped in a breath. "Yes. Yes, it was very nice."

"And it's late and time for you to catch some sleep. We both have work tomorrow." He pressed a kiss to her forehead and eased them apart.

With his mood and hopes lightened by that kiss, he slipped on his jacket and headed out into the damp, chilly night. At least the rain had cleared out.

One sizzling kiss was a fluke, two kisses were a strong hope, but this third kiss promised maybe, just maybe she was open to discovering if they could have a future together.

~*~

An auditorium of busily gabbing teachers couldn't distract Cami from ruminating over Jack's kisses. She was as giddy as a teen at the prospect of kissing him again, mixed with a hefty dose of fear and longing.

She brushed fingertips over her lips, still feeling the heat of his mouth on hers.

"Hi, Cami."

Pat's unexpected greeting sent Cami's heart pounding. She dropped her hand into her lap, curling her fingers guiltily around her coffee mug. "I need to put a bell on you. You caught me daydreaming."

Pat slid into the seat beside Cami and showed off comfortable-looking new shoes. "Blame my cushy new stealth shoes. You had a cat got the cream smile on your face, so, it must have been a great daydream. Did you have a good weekend?"

"Very busy and much accomplished."

"How's Mikki?"

"Uncomfortable, but momma and babies are all doing well."

"I'm so glad. Any progress with the yummy Jack?"

Heat rushed Cami.

Pat grinned. "Tell, tell. That blush promises good stuff."

"He kissed me, we kissed. Again. Twice." Three, really, if she counted that barely a kiss good night she'd given him on Saturday.

"Excellent."

Cami sighed. "They were very excellent kisses."

"Did he ask you out?"

"No, but I think he will. Only, I don't want to make another mistake. I don't want to be just another of his passing girlfriends. Neither of us have a good track record in lasting relationships."

"Stop right there. That's because you haven't met the right man at the right time. Jack might be the right one at the right time for you. Give it a shot."

"It's just so strange to consider dating him. He's been like family for so long, yet . . ."

"He's not family, he's a friend. You're both

single and clearly attracted to each other, what's the problem here?"

"Fear."

"Understandable after so many duds. So be upfront with Jack and talk. You already know him well, right? So instead of those pesky early dating learning-about-him questions, you can move on to the bigger issues. Ask him exactly what he wants from you. Does he want to be serious with you? Tell him what you want from him. Do you want to be serious with him? It sounds like you do, since you don't want to be just one of the girls. Go for it. Faint heart never won fair lady—well, in this case, yummy guy."

Cami laughed.

Fortunately, the workshop helped distract her and made the day fly by, and before long, she was free to head home. She'd enjoyed adding the walk to and from school to her daily exercise routine, and today was a particularly lovely walk, sunny and bright with a chill snap to the air and the trees splashing the town with festive gold, orange, and red.

After changing into comfortable clothes and starting a load of wash, she headed next door through the breezeway. She knocked on the door and opened it a crack. "Hi, I'm home."

"We're in the living room," Mikki called out over the bubbly music of Emily's television program.

As she walked through Mikki's kitchen, a tiny pink tornado crashed a hug around her legs and waved a big sheet of drawing paper. "Aunt Cami! Look! Look! I made a card! See my E!"

Emily held up the drawing paper filled with colorful marker and crayon scribbles and three distinct stick people, one with wild yellow scribble hair and a wobbly pink E underneath, one with a purple C, and one with three green lines that must be a K.

"You and your sisters, right?"

"That's me, that's Christie, and that's Kaylie. No hair for babies." Emily grabbed Cami's hand and tugged. "Let's sit with Mommy."

"Just a sec, sweetie. Mikki, do you need anything while I'm in the kitchen?"

"I'd love some applesauce and a glass of iced tea, thanks!"

Emily hopped into dancing around the kitchen and singing, "Applesauce, applesauce, applesauce, my applely, applely applesauce!"

"How was the in-service today?"

"Busy and noisy. Most of the workshop was a rehash of previous years, but I picked up a few useful new ideas, so worthwhile in the end. How was your day?"

"Did my best to imitate a beached whale and stay off my feet all day, except to pee—a lot—and make lunch."

Mikki set aside her knitting and took the glass and bowl. "Thanks. Emily's been a whirling dervish of energy, but a good girl for Mommy."

"I'm a good helper." Emily settled at the coffee table, scooped a bite of applesauce, and selected a clean sheet of paper.

"Yes, you are." Mikki sipped at her tea and groaned. "Oh, if only this had caffeine."

"Why don't you try to nap? Emily and I can

tackle some laundry for you."

"I would argue with you, but I'm too tired. A nap sounds wonderful. Thanks."

Unfortunately, the ordinary task of laundry left too much room for thinking and worrying over what she would do and say when she saw Jack again.

Shouldn't she be getting more cautious about relationships after so many failed ones? Shouldn't have all those failures taught her to act more circumspectly? While she craved more from him, she didn't want to be just another in the passing line of Jack's girls. Tumbling into a relationship with Jack as if he'd always been part of her life was too simple. Being in his arms was too easy.

She'd never dated a friend before. This was all so different and fast. What if it fizzled out like all the others, and he walked away, and then she had to see him dating others? If only all the what-ifs would stop spinning through her mind. Only, she was terrible at not stressing over important issues.

What if you give in to Pat's advice, stop stressing over possible outcomes, and just go with the flow? What if you just enjoy whatever Jack is willing to give? You aren't going to do anything foolish.

She sighed. Maybe that was one of her problems. She *never* did anything foolish.

~*~

Despite his frustrations with taking things slow and easy, Jack was enjoying the challenge of stealing time alone and kisses with Cami over the next few days. However, he needed to take the next step and ask her out on a proper, real-deal date before he ran out of sanity and reasons to stop in to fix or paint something for her.

Hell, go ahead and ask her. The worst that can happen is she shoots you down. Just go for it.

Ending his idiotic hesitation took until Thursday.

He watched the clock, aiming for her lunch break. Never had a minute hand moved so slowly. Jack grabbed his cell and dialed.

"Hi, Jack."

The relief at her picking up slammed a warm rush through him. "Hi, Cami." Say yes. Just say yes.

"This is a surprise."

"I had something to ask you, and thought I'd try to catch you on your lunch break. I'm not interrupting a meeting or anything, am I?"

Stop beating around the bush. You don't have all day here.

"No, just sitting here enjoying the quiet while I grade some homework and eat a sandwich. What's up?"

"Are you busy tomorrow night? I mean, as long as Mikki doesn't need you and the babies don't decide it's time, are you free?"

"Ah, no real plans at the moment." Measured curiosity filled her voice.

"Great. In that case, I know it's last minute, but would you like to have dinner and see a movie with me?"

"Are you asking me out on a date?" Amusement rang in her voice.

He laughed. "Which answer will get you to say yes?"

Cami's warm laughter raised his hopes. "I'm going to go out on a limb here and say yes."

"Then, yes, I am asking you out on a date."

"Okay. Just . . ."

Her pause knotted up his stomach like he'd never asked a woman out before. Well, maybe because asking had never mattered as much before.

"So long as nothing comes up with Mikki, it's a date."

His breath whooshed out. "Great. That's great. That's perfect."

"What time?"

"How about six? We can work out which movie between now and then. There are a couple good ones out. Your choice."

"Brave of you, considering one is a tearjerker chick flick."

"I'll bring the tissue box. However, I'm not worried because I'm sure you'll go for the cop show."

Her laughter rang out again. "I'll look at the paper tonight and pick one."

"Okay, I'll let you go."

"Have a good afternoon."

Yes, she said yes! He hung up, gave a fist pump, and spun around in his chair. Now, please let Mikki not go into labor in the next thirty-six hours.

His phone rang in his hand, and his heart jumped. Please, not Cami calling back with a conflict.

To his relief, the call was his mom. "Hi, Mom, what's up?"

"I hope this is an okay time to call, Jackie. I just wanted to say hi and check that you're still coming up on Sunday and not busy with helping Ray."

"I'm coming, don't worry."

"I was originally planning on a turkey, but I know you like grilled steak, so I was thinking of that, and your dad and I are going food shopping this afternoon."

"Either's fine."

"Pork chops are on sale too. So we could have those."

"Mom, whatever you feel like making is great by me. The weather looks good, so even if it's chilly we could use the grill if you decide on steak or chops. I'll bring wine and some dessert."

"Oh, don't bring any dessert. There'll be lots. The Thompsons are coming, they're headed down to Florida next Monday, so I wanted to have them over before they go, and the Riveras and the Perlmans are coming too."

So much for a quiet dinner with his parents. He grinned. "I'll bring three bottles."

"Wonderful. Also, if you could bring your toolbox?"

"What do you need fixed?"

"The living room ceiling fan just stopped working. I smelled smoke, but your dad said he didn't. So just in case, we've kept the wall switch off, and we bought a new fan this morning."

Oh, please, he didn't need either of them up on a ladder. Maybe he should bring four bottles of wine.

"Not a problem, I'll come up earlier than I planned then. Don't let Dad up on the ladder."

"Don't worry. With the cold snap, our arthritis is acting up too much to fiddle with screwdrivers and ladders. Only mid-October, and your dad is already threatening to move to Florida."

Jack laughed. "You'd like it down there, Mom. Maybe you and Dad should take a vacation, visit the Thompsons, and look for a small place so you don't have to deal with the cold anymore."

"But we'd be so far from you."

"I'd miss you too, but it's a quick plane trip, barely longer than my drive up to your house. So not a problem. I really believe you should give it a try."

He'd miss them if they became snowbirds like the Thompsons, but they were becoming so miserable with their aches and pains in the winter.

"Maybe . . ."

"Just consider it, Mom. You could rent a place. You don't need to buy. On Sunday, let's talk with the Thompsons and get some ideas. Okay?"

"Okay."

"Great. I'll be there early on Sunday with the wine and my toolbox."

"Love you, Jackie."

"Love you, too, Mom. Give Dad a hug for me."

He hung up and slumped back in his chair. He loved them to pieces, but seeing them getting older and slowing down was rough. Physically, they'd be much more comfortable somewhere with warm winters. Maybe he'd give them plane tickets for their Christmas present this year. Wouldn't hurt to help them explore the idea.

His phone rang again. Ray this time. His pulse sped. Please, please, please not Mikki in labor.

"Hey, Ray."

"Hi. Are you busy tomorrow after work?"

"Got a date. What did you need?"

"Oh, okay. Nothing that can't wait until the

weekend. Just needed a hand with the truck for a half hour or so. So a date, huh? Someone new?"

"Yes. First date."

"Well, good luck."

Jack grinned. "Thanks." With Cami's yes, his luck was already turning to the good.

Chapter Five

*C*AMI SNATCHED ONE LAST LOOK IN THE MIRROR. Okay, yes, her favorite dressy purple sweater and gray slacks were the right choice for her date with Jack. She added lipstick, scrubbed most of it off, and then put it back on.

A date. A real date with Jack. Unaccountably nervous, she felt like a teen sneaking out with the boy her parents didn't want her seeing. She'd only mentioned in passing to Mikki that she was going to the movies, not with whom.

Ready as she could be, she grabbed her purse and coat and headed next door with a brief, guilty look over her shoulder. Silly, since Mikki, Ray, and Emily were tucked safely away inside and very unlikely to catch her leaving with Jack.

Several blocks away from home, Jack glanced at her, frowning. "What's the matter? Is Mikki okay?"

She gathered a long breath. Time to do a better

job of relaxing. "Sorry, Mikki's fine. I'm just still a little preoccupied and slow to wind down after a long, busy week. TGIF. I needed this night out. Thanks."

"You're welcome. Between school and home, you've been working hard."

"True. However, I did have an excellent moment today. One of my students, who's been really struggling with reading, read me a whole sentence today. I nearly fell out of my chair I was so happy."

"Aw, that's awesome."

"You could just see the light bulb go off, and she was grinning ear to ear."

"Those light bulb moments are the best. So, did you decide on which movie? Cops? Tissues?"

She laughed. "Neither."

"Please, not the dancing bunnies."

"Nope. I get to see that one with Emily. I decided I'm in the mood for the spy thriller with the over-the-top stunts and pyrotechnics."

He laughed. "Thank you!"

"So, I picked the movie, where did you choose for supper?"

"I found this small place up in Belmar that does great steaks and fresh seafood. They make a roasted potato side that you absolutely have to taste."

The restaurant was small, casual, and comfortable. They both ordered a glass of wine and nibbled on the fresh-baked sourdough rolls while they studied the menu.

Cami took another roll from the basket. "These rolls are so good. I could make a meal of them."

Jack chose the porterhouse steak, roasted

potatoes, and house salad, and convinced Cami to try the filet and shrimp combo. After the waiter left with their order, their conversation faltered.

She chewed over Pat's instructions to ask Jack exactly what he wanted. Simple, but difficult.

After a swallow of wine, Jack gave her a steady gaze with those intense blue eyes of his as if he had serious thoughts of his own percolating. "What are you thinking?"

She decided to be honest. "Oh, just how odd it is to be on a first date with someone I've known for so long." And, yes, she held back her thoughts of how her body hummed and warmed when he looked at her like that.

He nodded. "I know what you mean."

She couldn't just sit and stare at him. Unready to ask the important questions, she scrambled for a simple one. "So, tell me something I don't know about you."

"Hmm." His brows narrowed for a long moment, and then a grin lit his face. "When I was a kid, I had a cat, Charlie, with seven toes on each of his front paws, and he had a mustache-shaped black streak under his nose. He was the best cat. I'd toss him treats, and he'd catch them in the air between his paws. How about you? What's something I don't know about you?"

"I would have liked a cat. I used to ask Santa for one regularly when I was small."

"Your parents always had dogs, right?"

"Yes. And I like dogs, but I just always wanted a cat that would curl in my lap and keep me company."

"You could have a cat now. Why not?"

"Too many no-pet apartments. But, true, now that I'm living here, I could have one. Maybe one of these days, once life settles down. Why don't you have a cat now yourself?"

"To be honest? No idea. Maybe we should both check out the next adoption day at the pet store."

"Maybe." Coming home to something that was her own and happy to see her would be nice. "So, what else don't I know about you?"

Jack wrinkled his brow. "This is harder than it seems. We've known each other for years. I'm probably an open book to you by now."

"Okay, let's try an embarrassing childhood moment?"

"Hmm. Okay, here's something goofy from when I was a kid. When I was eight, I professed my undying love to Betsy MacKinnon on Valentine's Day. She shot me down in flames and kissed Dirk Smith."

"Aw."

"Looking back, I suspect it might have been the plan for four kids that did me in. Plus, Dirk played it smart and just asked her to go ice skating."

"Four kids?" Her wishful thinking perked up at that little detail.

"Seemed like a good idea at the time."

After their laughter settled, Jack grinned. "Okay, your turn. Any embarrassing childhood moments for you?"

"Oh, yes. I had a disastrous Valentines' Day once as well. I was thirteen."

He let loose a groaning chuckle. "Thirteen was a bad age."

"Oh, yes. Anyhow, back when we were kids,

Mikki and I were very close in looks and we had fun with our twinness. I was crazy about Robby Delvecchio, he was really sweet, and I thought he liked me. Then came Valentine's Day and the truth was exposed. He liked Mikki, but wasn't always certain who was who, so he'd played it safe all year and schmoozed with both of us. Mikki gave him back his chocolate heart and told him to get glasses and a brain."

"What a dope."

"Looking back, it's funny, but, boy, it hurt at the time. That's when Mikki and I stopped trying to look alike and started just being ourselves. It was a good lesson."

Their meals arrived and, as they ate, Jack switched their game over. "Let's try favorite/least favorite now, and see if we know each other as well as we think. Ask me a question."

"Okay. Should be fun. What's my favorite color?"

"Easy. Purple. By the way, I really like that sweater on you."

"Thanks. And your favorite color is blue, but you like dark blue better than light blue."

"True. Now let's try something harder. The vegetable I like the least."

"Cauliflower, unless it's drowned in cheese."

"Hey, you're good at this. The only vegetable you hate is Brussels sprouts, but Mikki likes them, and your mom always mixes up who likes them and who doesn't."

Cami grinned. "The bane of my life, those sprouts. Okay, since we're seeing a movie tonight, favorite classic movie. Yours is Casablanca."

"That one never gets old. Your favorite is North by Northwest."

This game kept them laughing and reminiscing all through the meal and the drive to the movie. The spy thriller was way over the top, as expected, but the good cast and smart dialogue helped suspend disbelief and had them scoring it a 4.5 out of 5 on the ride home.

It was after midnight, and lights were out next door when Jack pulled into his driveway.

"I had a wonderful time tonight." She hadn't asked the important questions that still pricked at her mind but she also hadn't relaxed and laughed so much in ages.

He grinned. "So did I. Think you'd be up to doing this again?"

"I think we could." She fished her keys from her purse.

"Good. I'm looking forward to it." He slipped his hand into hers and squeezed gently. "I'll walk you to your door."

He caught her hand as they walked down the driveway and around the hedge. The air was crisp and the stars bright.

Now came the awkward part. Her nerves hummed. The hour was far too late to ask him in for coffee or dessert. Did they end the evening like friends with an ordinary, casual hug or like a real date with a deliberate kiss?

~*~

Jack waited as Cami unlocked her door, wanting to kiss her and take her in his arms. He tucked his hands in his jacket pockets. What did he do on a first date when he felt as if they'd always been together?

She opened the door and faced him with a nervous smile. "Well . . . good night." She brushed a kiss over his mouth.

That decided him.

He slid a hand over her jaw, keeping her close, their mouths meeting in a warm and easy kiss.

Cami wrapped an arm around his waist, sighing a sweet "Yes."

Still kissing, they stepped inside. She pressed a hand to the door and shut it against the chill night. Only one dim light lit the living room, leaving her small foyer shadowy and inviting.

That kiss ignited another kiss, and another, each too good to resist taking the next. Stepping blindly as they shed coats, he lost himself in the heated kisses, until his legs hit a living room chair.

He sank into the seat, carrying Cami along to straddle his lap. Kisses deepened, hot and wet, hurried and hungry, inciting a need for more and more contact. He gripped her rear, loving the pleasurable ache of her weight against him as they rode and rocked together.

Cami tugged at his shirt, freeing the shirttails from his khakis, and then her bare hands were gliding over his bare skin.

He groaned and slid his hands under her sweater, taking a long moment to savor the smooth heat of her waist, torn between taking all the time he could and greedily indulging in every sensation.

She raised her arms, breaking the kiss just long enough to let him sweep the purple fluff up and off. A lavender satin bra cupped the full curves of her breasts, and her silky blond hair spilled around her shoulders.

She took his breath away. Yes, he'd seen her in swimsuits, but tonight changed everything he imagined he knew. Looking into her dark brown eyes and drinking in the sight of her, he skimmed his hands over her warm skin and fondled her satin-covered breasts, and she shivered under his touch.

"Oh, Cami, you're beautiful." He dragged off his shirt. There, more skin to skin, much better. His cock ached, but his khakis were staying zipped until he had his head clear on where they were going here.

They sank back into kissing and exploring with hands and mouths.

He caressed down to her bra's front clasp. "May I?" He glanced up.

"Yes."

He unfastened the bra and filled his hands with the warm weight of her breasts, soft, perfect handfuls. How he wanted to taste those tightly pearled, sensitive nipples.

A vague responsible thought poked through his sensual haze: this only and no further tonight.

Right. Slow down. Slow. If this is right, you have the rest of your life to explore loving Cami.

He traced his fingers over her, delaying the pleasure of taking those beautiful breasts into his mouth. Shivers ran through Cami at each stroke.

He returned his focus to kisses, to relaxed and steady caresses. They'd already gone far further than he'd hoped when he first kissed her this evening. He'd been waiting since the day they'd first met to have Cami in his arms, six long years, and he refused to mess up this night in a greedy rush.

"Sorry it took so long." He trailed kisses over

her throat, discovering sensitive places below her ears.

She arched her neck back as she shivered and gasped. "What?"

"For us to be together. Sorry our timing never worked. Sorry we missed this together for so long."

Cami tensed. "Jack." A rougher shudder ran through her. "We have to keep this just between ourselves."

"Huh?" The oddness of what she'd said trickled into his brain, and he paused his kisses.

She shivered again and leaned back, pressing her hands to his chest. "If we get into a relationship."

If? From where he sat, with Cami straddling his lap, his erection straining at his zipper, and her bare breasts playing a tempting hide and seek behind the silk curtain of her hair, they already were into a relationship.

"It's not just us that it affects . . ."

What? This was a bad time to talk and expect his brain to be fully engaged beyond what her body was doing with his.

"They worry too much about me. Mikki says I'm always getting involved with the wrong men."

The change from pleasure to panic in her eyes cleared his head. She was really worried. He'd missed something in the conversation.

"Tell me exactly what you mean." He sucked in a harsh breath, struggling to see why she was worried. What was happening between them was all pretty simple. They were both unattached, both interested in each other, and both free and clear to explore this intense connection.

"Brent breaking things off with me upset Mikki. I don't want her worrying about anything but herself right now. She could have the twins any day now."

That bit he could understand. Mikki's official due date might be November 10th, but the babies would arrive on their own schedule.

"My parents, they'll think I'm rushing into this too quickly after Brent."

"Okay." Right, parents always worried.

"And Ray's your friend and my friend, and if something went wrong, this could put him in the middle."

That he also got. Hadn't he had a similar argument with himself?

"Emily, she'd be hurt the most if something went wrong between us. If Brent leaving me hurt her, think what a problem between *us* would do."

True, Emily was far too young to understand people leaving or relationships breaking apart. Just because he had every intention of making this relationship work, that he wanted to make it permanent, didn't mean that he would succeed. He'd seen great relationships and marriages crash and burn. All he could do is promise he'd do his best.

He nodded. "I get that." He rubbed her tense shoulders. "So, what are you wanting to do?"

"Because of all of that, that's why, I think, we should just keep this, us, quiet between us."

He let out his breath. At least she wasn't backing off. However, her wanting to keep him a secret rankled. "So you want us to be some secret affair."

She jolted, those beautiful bedroom eyes

widening in confusion. "I—I just . . . no, just quiet, just not public for now. Until we're sure what's happening here."

"What's happening here seems clear and a good thing, not something to hide."

"It is. A very good thing." She sighed and slumped into his embrace, her warm cheek pressed against his shoulder. "I just can't give them more to worry about. Not right now."

"Okay." Agreeing bothered him, but he was unwilling to risk his hopes for a future with Cami by taking a hard stand on his opinions. He'd play it by ear. "For now."

"I had a good time tonight. Thank you." She looked up, a rueful smile on her lips. "A wonderful time."

"Me too. We'll keep this low key in public, but I like what we have going here." He stroked his hand through her hair and pressed a kiss to her mouth. "It's late. I should let you get some sleep. I want to see you tomorrow. Okay?" He fastened her bra.

"Yes, I'll see you tomorrow. I'm sorry."

He draped her sweater around her shoulders. "Don't be sorry. I want to know what's on your mind. It's important we talk. I had a great time this evening, and I plan on having great dreams tonight." He took a short kiss and caressed her breast. "I have some amazing inspiration to work with." He grinned. "Dream of me too?"

Cami laughed. "Maybe."

Her sweet, fierce kiss goodnight at the door kept him motivated and warm as he walked home through the chilly dark. Yeah, with kisses like that, he could deal with her request to lay low in public for a while.

And he looked forward to all the ways he could work on convincing Cami they were meant to be together.

~*~

Once Jack reached his front door, Cami let the drape fall shut and groaned. Oh, boy, they'd gotten carried away. Dinner and a movie, that's all she'd had in her plans for the evening, and yes, maybe a kiss or two. But kissing and being kissed senseless and ending up half-dressed in his lap and enjoying every incendiary moment . . . definitely beyond her wildest expectation of this evening, perfect and wonderful.

Until she'd started thinking too much.

She stared at the sweater clutched in her hand. Was wishing he'd stayed really so terrible?

This grinding need for *more* totally clashed with her need to slow down and keep this whatever was happening between them low key. They had to, until she was sure. Well, more sure. Until the babies came, and Mikki and Ray were too distracted to worry over her, and life settled down.

However, she'd agreed to see him again tomorrow. So much for slow. She glanced at the clock. Make that today.

Dream of me, he'd said. Immediately, fresh heat rolled through her with the echoing sensation of his kisses.

Oh, dreaming of Jack would be no problem at all.

After a night of tossing and turning between those dreams, more composure came with the sunrise. Even if she were really making a mistake, even if this was just a reaction to breaking up with Brent, being in Jack's arms last night had felt like finding an answer to an unsolvable question. Despite her confusion, she'd loved every moment with Jack before her panic derailed the pleasure.

If only Mikki hadn't been so adamant that Jack was a bad match for her. She wasn't willing to stop seeing him, and she wasn't willing to come clean to Mikki how much she wanted to explore this new relationship with Jack. How did she trust her feelings *and* trust her sister with such conflicting input?

At the moment, that left her stuck with the awkward and unsatisfactory compromise of sneaking around.

She puttered all morning unpacking and arranging her bedroom. She'd promised to have lunch with Mikki, but she dreaded heading over. Being unable to share her worries and questions with Mikki left her confused. She'd never shared every last detail with Mikki about her relationships—there were some TMI boundaries they didn't cross—but they'd always been able to discuss the guys in their lives and share advice. This deliberately concealing a new man in her life felt weird.

Only, what if Mikki *was* right and Jack *was* the wrong kind of guy for her? He was definitely the opposite of Brent. Romance with Brent had been comfortable and sensible.

She groaned and headed for the door. Comfortable, sensible, and ultimately frustrating and unfulfilling.

Being with Jack was wild, crazy, and wonderful.

Plenty of zing. Being with Jack was also frustrating and nerve wracking, but brimming with the potential of being incredibly fulfilling.

Helping Mikki with housework and lunch worked as a welcome distraction, until they'd settled at the kitchen table with their sandwiches and soup.

"So you were out last night? On a date?"

Cami panicked. "Uh, no. Uh, just went to a movie."

"Oh, you and Pat? Was it good?"

Cami swallowed a mouthful of tea and nodded, hating to lie.

The phone rang, Mikki answered, and it was Mom, saving Cami from having to lie any more about last night.

The afternoon slipped peacefully by, Ray arrived home from the hardware store, and Jack joined them. The guys worked on Ray's truck for a time, and then everyone settled in the living room to hang out while waiting on supper.

Ray's cell phone rang. He frowned at the screen. "Sorry, it's work. Got to answer this." He took the call out in the quieter kitchen.

He returned a few minutes later and sank onto the couch next to Mikki with a groan. "I have to work next Saturday. At least Morgan gave me notice, but damn, I was taking Emily pumpkin picking then, and she's been so excited about seeing the farm animals and getting to ride a pony. Sunday's no good. It's supposed to pour."

"I can take her." Cami and Jack both spoke at once.

Jack grinned, his eyes glinting with mirth. "How

about we both do it? It'll be fun. I haven't done the hayride and pumpkin picking thing in ages, and we've babysat Emily together before."

"Oh, okay." Anyhow, pumpkin picking with a three-year old should be a safe and innocent outing. What possibly could go wrong?

Jack scooped up Emily, who squealed with giggles. "It's a date."

"Thanks, guys, we owe you."

Despite the ordinary evening, like so many evenings in the past, being near Jack was suddenly so awkward. The same old smiles held new layers of meaning. Accidental touches, once so innocent, promised fascinating adventures ahead. Resisting responding to him and the impulses of her desires was hard. She couldn't help recalling every lovely moment of last night, his kisses, sitting in his lap, or how good she'd felt in his hands.

By the time Mikki gave in and headed up to bed, Cami was completely on edge. Her own fault. She'd built up unrealistic expectations around his statement *I want to see you tomorrow.* That could be interpreted a number of ways, but apparently not the way her heart had read his words.

Her heart?

Great, yes, she was already emotionally involved. Couldn't she for once explore a possible relationship without jumping in with her emotions before it was safe to do so?

Annoyed with herself, Cami said her good nights all around, hoping her voice sounded like every ordinary night before.

Jack and Ray waved, barely breaking their attention on the game.

Two big boys. She shook her head and headed home through the breezeway, full of relief and disappointment.

After washing her face and changing into her pajamas, she felt at loose ends. It was too early for bed, so she'd make a cup of the cinnamon apple tea and read for a bit. She started the kettle and set up the coffee maker for the morning.

Her cell phone whistled for an incoming text.

Jack: I didn't want to scare you by knocking, but I'm at your backdoor.

She turned.

He waved at her in the dark.

She winced at her flannel snowman pajamas. Completely decent, considering he'd already seen her bare breasts yesterday, but not exactly what she wanted Jack to catch her wearing.

Her phone whistled again.

Jack: Cute pj's.

She laughed and let him in, grateful he'd come to her kitchen door, which faced the fence and his house. "I didn't expect you."

He pressed a kiss to her lips. "I told you I wanted to see you. That means *you*, without friends and family. Just you."

The teakettle began its rolling vibration and first wisps of a whistle.

"I was making tea. Apple cinnamon. Would you like some?"

"Sure. I'll try it." He hung his jacket on the hook and rubbed his hands together. "It's not supposed to freeze tonight, but the temperature really dropped, and the wind's got a bite."

"Tea will warm you up then."

"But first, this." He pulled her close into a sweet and leisurely kiss, and she was plenty warm when he stepped away.

They carried the mugs out to the living room. Jack solved the issue of where and how they would sit by tugging her down with him onto the couch. After kicking off his shoes, he flicked the throw blanket over them both and cuddled her to him. "Ah, that's better."

He took a testing sip of his tea. "Hey, this tastes good. Like apple pie, sort of."

"It's one of my favorites."

He settled his arm around her more comfortably and picked up the television remote. "Anything you feel like watching?"

"At this time of night? No, I usually channel surf until a show catches my interest. If you want to watch the end of the ball game, go ahead."

"You sure?"

"I like baseball too. And it's more fun to watch with company."

She might not have watched the game if she was alone, but he enjoyed baseball, and he could have chosen to finish watching the game with Ray.

"Thanks." He clicked over to the game, just in time to see a great double play. "Yes!"

"That was amazing. They make throwing the ball like that look so simple."

Sitting cozily with Jack under the blanket and watching the final innings was a delightful way to end her day, and her earlier nerves disappeared.

The game ended on an exciting bases-loaded, two-out hit that had them both holding their breaths.

"Yes! World Series, here we come." Jack gave her a high-five and grinned. "And Ray now owes me a six pack. I told him they'd pull off the win!"

"What a great game! I'm glad we watched it."

Simmering heat filled his blue eyes, and he stroked a lock of hair behind her ear.

Wanting just as much, she pressed her lips to his.

This time, settling into a kiss was easy. Brushing lips together, playful and lazy, she savored the warmth of his mouth, testing various slides of lips, nibbles, flicks of tongue, and tender bites.

They shifted together, stretching out to recline on their sides. Being together felt so familiar, easy and comfortable. He stroked her back and down to her bottom, holding her close. At his teasing lick and murmur, she opened her mouth to him and a luscious kiss. His light, exploring caresses over her breast raised tingling shivers and she wished he'd slip his hand beneath her pajama top.

Still only kissing, still dressed, they shifted again until she lay beneath him, cradling him between her legs. Oh, this felt even better, the firm weight of him and lovely deep kisses so right, full of the same rich heat of last night, but without the craziness. She'd never been so thoroughly kissed, and she loved every moment of the pleasuring, leisurely rock of their bodies together, melting under the hard press of him against her center.

Jack groaned and sat back abruptly, jarring her from her sensual haze.

What?

After a heavy indrawn breath, he smiled apologetically, eyes full of warm longing. "It's late. I need to be responsible and head home."

A wild urge to blurt "No, stay," surged in her throat, but he was right. She nodded. She should be glad he was being responsible. After last night, caution was the right course until they were both completely sure about this relationship.

"I'll be away all day at my parents tomorrow, but I'll call you in the evening. Okay?"

"I'd like that."

He stroked her cheek before standing and tucked the blanket over her. "Sleep well."

One last brief kiss and then he was gone.

Cami lay there for a time afterward, adrift in longing, stunned how much she missed his arms around her. Oh, yes, she might be unsure, but she'd definitely leapt in headlong with her heart.

Please, please don't let this be another mistake.

Chapter Six

*J*ACK LOVED HIS PARENTS, BUT HIS DAY WITH THEM dragged on excruciatingly. The new fan installation went smoothly, but unfortunately, they had no other chores to keep him busy. If only he had a brother or sister to deflect attention or give him someone his own age to talk to. If only he'd brought Cami . . .

His parents' friends' arrival didn't help. They were all nice people, but when they weren't grilling him on his life, they were talking grandchildren, retirement issues, ailments and doctors, and local gossip, and he could only handle snacking on so much cheese and crackers while waiting for supper. These gatherings always ran late, so he wouldn't be home until at least midnight, far too late to stop by and see Cami.

His efforts during supper to shift the

conversation and his parents' thoughts to considering Florida at least part-time met with some success. The Thompsons were thrilled with the idea of showing them around.

After supper, he jumped to help Mom clear the plates, and while the group was relocating to the game table in the family room, he slipped out to the porch for a moment of quiet, caving to the temptation to check in with Cami.

In case she was still at Ray and Mikki's, he sent her a text.

How's your evening going?

Safe enough wording.

She answered immediately.

Cami: Just walked into my place. Parents just went home.

Jack: Mine are about to serve up dessert.

Cami: Anything good?

Jack: Pumpkin pie, magic cookie bars, something Mrs. Thompson made with a ton of whipped topping, and Mom's chocolate cake.

Cami: Sounds yummy, but sugar overload.

Jack: I'll bring you some. Mom will load me up with leftovers when I head home. I have to recommend the chocolate cake.

Cami: I do like chocolate.

They shared bits of their day and this simple connection made him ridiculously happy.

"Jackie, I need you to reach me the cake stand down from the shelf."

"Be right there, Mom."

Jack: Time for cake and cards. See you tomorrow.

Cami: ☺ Have fun.

He retrieved the glass cake stand from the top

pantry shelf.

Mom immediately filled his hands with cake plates. "Oh, Jackie, I meant to tell you. I tried calling you Friday night, but you must have been out."

"You didn't leave a message."

Mom waved her hand. "Oh, it wasn't important."

"You could have called my cell."

"If you were on a date, I didn't want to bother you. The computer wasn't working, and your father was busy out in the garage. But then, all of a sudden, all by myself, I got it to work! I was so proud of myself."

Dad collected the coffee cups onto a tray. "So, were you out on a date?"

"I was."

Shit. Jack snapped his mouth closed. Maybe Cami hadn't meant the keeping things quiet to extend to his family and parents' friends, but thoughtlessly blurting stuff was poor practice.

Mom smiled expectantly. "A nice girl?"

He laughed. "Mom, they're all nice girls. Why date them otherwise?"

"Don't be a wise aleck. So tell us about her."

"She's gorgeous and smart. She's a teacher at another school, but I've known her for a while. Friday was our first date, so early days."

They grilled him thoroughly, but he managed to sidestep her identity, and the more he talked about Cami, the more he couldn't wait to see her again.

"I'm so glad you've met someone who makes you look so happy. Angela, well, she was vivacious, but she wasn't the one for you. You need someone who's more than just decorative. Someone like Cami

Alexander, for instance. We've always liked her."

He suppressed a laugh. Oh, Mom, if you only knew.

"You're not getting any younger you know." Dad gave him a teasing frown.

"If she's the one, Jackie, I have your grandmother's ring. It's a lovely platinum setting with a very nice diamond. I know she'd want you to have it."

"Geez, Mom! Let me talk her into a second date before you go planning our engagement."

Dad just laughed.

However, Jack remembered the ring, and it would look perfect on Cami's hand. Years ago when he'd believed Janine was the woman for him, they hadn't offered him Grandma's ring.

Something to ponder.

For the first time since Janine, he wanted to wear his heart on his sleeve for all to see.

Mom patted his cheek. "Never too soon to start thinking ahead."

"We'd like to be grandparents before we're too old and decrepit to enjoy it."

"Dad!"

They were having too much fun teasing him to let up as they set the table for dessert, their friends joined in, and the good-natured, embarrassing ribbing continued until Mom declared it time for cards.

The evening crawled by over coffee, dessert, and endless rounds of pinochle, but his parents were happy, and he liked making them happy.

After the last of Mom and Dad's friends headed home, he helped clean up and loaded the leftover desserts into his truck. He hugged Mom and Dad goodnight, but Mom followed him outside.

"Mom, it's cold out. You should stay inside."

"Dad and I talked, Jackie, and we decided you should take this now." She slipped a small box into his hand and kissed his cheek. "For luck. Just in case. For when the moment is right."

"Thanks, Mom." He tucked the ring box into his pocket and hugged her close.

"Drive safely, and give me two rings on the phone when you get in so I can sleep."

He grinned. "I always do. I will. Love you."

The long drive home along the Parkway gave him plenty of time for reflection.

Nine years ago, he and Janine had both made mistakes in their relationship from the start. He'd been madly, stupidly, blindly in love back then. Making mistakes was so easy when you were young. He liked to believe he'd learned a thing or two from his mistakes during their unhappy two years together, but maybe he'd taken those lessons too much to heart. Since Janine, he'd let none of the women he'd dated close enough for them to hurt him. He'd let none of them close enough to feel more deeply than desire and friendship.

Somehow, Cami had slipped through his every defense. Maybe it was simply the passage of time and, hopefully, some maturity, but his feelings for Cami were so different from how he'd felt for Janine.

Yes, now was far too soon to act on the ring sitting in his pocket. By the way she'd panicked the other night, Cami was far from ready, but having her in his life felt so right, he hated wasting a minute of the time they could spend together.

When he pulled into his garage, he sat for a minute in the quiet, wearily wide-awake from too much caffeine and sugar, and then gave Mom her two rings on the phone.

As he tucked the desserts in the refrigerator, his cell phone rang. Cami's name on the screen gave him a surge of happy energy.

"Hey, Cami. You're up late. Everything okay?"

"I was reading. I was about to turn in when I saw your headlights, so I thought I'd say goodnight."

"I'm glad you called." He fished the ring box from his pocket and hung his jacket in the closet.

"Did you have a good time at your parents'?"

"Yes and, as threatened, I brought home a bagful of desserts. I'll bring some by tomorrow." He turned out the light and headed down the hall to his bedroom.

"I made beef stew for our supper tomorrow. There's plenty if you'd like to join us."

"I'd like that." They'd shared uncounted meals together over at Ray and Mikki's, but this was the first time Cami had extended the invitation.

"Okay, I'll let you go. Sleep well."

Maybe he was over-reading the warmth in her voice, but happiness filled him. "You too. Have a good day at work tomorrow."

He set aside his phone and studied the time-yellowed white leather box. He pressed the tiny button latch and the lid sprang open. Nestled in blue velvet, the diamond sparkled in its platinum setting. Would Cami be shocked if she knew what he was contemplating or how fast the pure rightness of the decision had hit him?

He snapped the lid shut and set the box in the top dresser drawer. Time to exercise some more patience.

~*~

Cami was on her walk to school, enjoying the brisk, sunny morning, when a short horn beep and a familiar "Hey, Cami!" rang out.

She turned, filled with a happy thrill, as Jack pulled up to the curb.

"Want a lift?" His smile seemed warmer than usual.

Spending a few minutes with him was so tempting . . .

"Thanks, but no. I'm enjoying my walk and the good weather."

"What time's supper?"

"I think we'll eat around six, as usual."

"Okay, good. That leaves me time to hit the gym after school. I'll see you then."

"Have a good day."

"You, too." He waved and drove off.

A busy school day kept her mind mostly occupied, with only an occasional meander into daydreaming. Once home, she dove into her chores and exercise, followed by a long relaxing shower where she let herself indulge in very pleasant daydreams of Jack's caresses and kisses. And, yes, he was definitely in her thoughts as she chose her underwear, jeans, and a silky-soft burnt orange cardigan sweater.

The breezeway was still toasty warm from the sunny day as she headed next door, and Mikki's kitchen window was wide open. Cami set the heavy stew pot and loaf of bread on the iron patio chair and raised her hand to knock.

". . . Jack ever going to settle down?"

At Mikki's question, Cami froze.

Ray gave a sad laugh. "I think he gave up on that when Janine dumped him a year before you and I met. Frankly, he was lucky to lose her, but the break up was ugly. He took it hard and became the commitment-phobic eternal bachelor we know. I'm surprised he kept Angela around as long as he did."

Who was Janine? Her heart went out to Jack.

"Well, Angela never seemed the settle-down type either. Maybe the next one will be the one for him."

Ray sighed. "I doubt it. I don't know how he deals with it. It's not like we're in college anymore. Makes me tired just thinking about his revolving door of dating."

"You've become an old fart. Don't men like the idea of dating a bunch of women?"

"Hey, that's happy old fart to you. Fantasize? Yes. Really want? Not so much." His laughter deepened into sensual teasing.

Cami waited for a lull in the subsequent lovey-dovey murmurs and some giggles from Mikki before she knocked on the door. "Hi, ready for some supper?"

After more low laughter, Mikki called out, "Come on in!"

Cami found Mikki and Ray sitting at the kitchen table looking flushed.

"I hope you don't mind, but I invited Jack to join us. I made more than enough stew and bread. He's bringing us some desserts from his parents' party yesterday."

"When did you talk to Jack today?"

She set the pot on the stove and set the dial on low to warm the stew. "He passed me on my walk to school. Shouldn't you be on the couch with your feet up, not fussing in the kitchen?"

"I had to pee and I'm just taking a break here on my way back to my beached status. I'm so tired of lying around."

"Just a few more weeks and you'll be complaining to me how tired you are and wishing you could lie down."

"Totally true, but I'm still tired of lying around *now*. All I'm doing these days is sitting, eating, and needing to pee every five minutes from the pumpkins bouncing on my bladder."

Cami scooped up Mikki's glass. "Come on, shoo, back to the living room. Come on, Ray, tell her."

Ray handed Cami a glass of wine. "I tried already."

Mikki finally submitted to their nagging, and they settled in the living room where Emily was playing with her dolls in front of the television.

Jack showed up right on time, bearing desserts, and looking tasty himself in his blue plaid flannel shirt and jeans.

Mikki waved. "Jack! Finally, the twins and I are starving. Now that you're here, we can eat."

Jack laughed. "Good thing I took a short shower."

Jack and Ray volunteered to help Cami serve up supper.

"Hey, Cami, meant to tell you." Ray opened a new bottle of merlot. "I was talking to Brenda Bell today, and she happened to mention her brother-in-law Martin was looking to meet someone nice. Brenda wanted to know if you'd like to meet him. He's a CPA, just bought a house in Bayhead, and is apparently really smart and nice. What do you think?"

Jack stilled in his gathering the flatware.

She cringed inside. Could you say major awkward moment? "Tell Brenda thanks for me, but I'm not quite ready."

"I heard that." Mikki waddled into the kitchen. "Come on, Cami. What would one date hurt? You need to jump back in the dating pool eventually."

Jack plucked another plate from the rack. "I've met Marty. He's a real nice guy. "

Oh, not helping here, Jack. She couldn't help turning and giving him a glare.

He kept a poker face, but his blue eyes twinkled.

She finished turning, smiling calmly at Mikki. "Eventually, yes. But I just want to take a break, focus on you, family, and getting through the holidays. Go sit. I'll bring your supper."

"I thought you wanted to meet someone new."

"I do. Eventually. We'll see what the new year brings. Just not right now."

Mikki and Ray kept pushing all through supper, so she gave in. "I'll think about it, okay?"

They all called it an early evening after dessert. Emily was already tucked in, Mikki was tired, and it was a school night for Cami and Jack after all.

An early night worked for Cami. Fighting the tension of desire with no way to ease the need was exhausting and the three glasses of wine had done nothing to relax her. The ordinary, accidental touches, even the simple brush of fingers as they passed a plate at supper left her on edge and feeling snappish.

"Good night, everybody." Jack pulled on his jacket, his face perfectly innocent. "Cami, I'll carry that pot over to your place on my way."

"Okay, thanks." She hugged Mikki and Ray and opened the breezeway door. Jack hefted the stew pot, and they set off for her place.

"This breezeway sure is handy for you."

"I love being able to run next door without a coat. Ray's looking at ways to put up storm windows so it can be more of a three-season room than just a hallway. It gets so much sun, but those old louvered windows are drafty."

"That's a good idea."

Jack tucked the pot in her fridge and turned, his face stern. "I've been dying to do this all evening." He tugged her into his arms and seized a fierce, urgent kiss. "Don't go out with Marty."

"Jealous?"

She'd never seen so much heat flare in his ice-blue eyes.

"Yes! And yes, damn it, he's a nice guy. A great guy. But, I don't want you going out with him. *Anyone.*"

The urge to tease him tempted her for a moment, but she spoke the truth. "Why would I need to when I have a perfectly nice guy right here in my kitchen?"

"I'm not feeling all that nice." The growl in his voice as he rasped kisses down her throat filled her with delicious shivers.

"You feel very nice to me." She slid her hands

down his back, his flannel shirt soft and warm over firm muscle, gripped his hips, and rose up to meet him for another kiss.

Yes, this consuming need was crazy. Yes, giving into this desire was undoubtedly very foolish and probably leading her to making other great mistakes ahead. But never had she launched into a mistake that felt so good.

He ran his hands over her rear, pulling her even closer. If only his hands were on her bare skin. If only her hands were—

No. She needed to be sensible and careful. Hadn't her heart been bruised enough recently? Jack could hurt her so easily. She'd been so topsy-turvy since learning he'd broken up with Angela and even more so since that first kiss. And, judging by the wrench she'd felt at overhearing his past heartache, her feelings were rapidly growing into much more.

"Ask me to stay for a while," he murmured at her ear, and then nipped at her lobe, tugging gently.

Oh, that was a dangerous request. Agreeing wasn't at all sensible.

But she was so desperately sick of sensible. She was tired of worrying over right and proper when all it did was leave her alone with her hollow heart, unloved and lonely. She was tired of a lonesome, empty bed. She was tired of silent, solitary nights and mornings without conversation.

So stop thinking, stop worrying. Just enjoy now.

Oh, yes. Enjoy this sweet, intense kiss he swept her into without waiting for her answer. Enjoy the strength of his arms around her and inquiring press of his aroused body. Enjoy the warm, clean scent of him. Enjoy how good they were together *now*. Time enough tomorrow, later to dissect the complications.

If ever she were to be foolish, she wanted to be foolish with Jack. "Stay . . . please."

Without breaking his kisses, he shrugged out of his jacket and tossed it over a kitchen chair. He slipped his hands under her sweater and lightly stroked the bare skin of her waist, stirring up luscious shivers.

"Oh, that's so good." She nibbled at his mouth and brushed her lips along his jaw, enjoying every mesmerizing caress.

Fresh kisses heated, hurried, and deepened as he backed her through the kitchen toward the dim living room. Colliding with the wall halted them in place.

"I was thinking about you all day. Completely distracted," he said roughly. He rubbed his smooth cheek to hers. He'd shaved along with his shower. "I could hardly wait for supper to be over."

Cami laughed. "And they kept talking and talking over dessert."

"All I wanted for dessert was you."

He slid his fingers into her hair, finding and discarding the pins and band securing the chignon, and combed her hair free, massaging her scalp. She sighed for the pleasure of his simple touch.

After another long kiss, next he worked at her cardigan buttons, slowly sliding the sweater away and revealing her breasts in the thin ivory lace bra.

He groaned and dipped his head to close the wet heat of his mouth over her nipple, rasping his tongue across the lace and taut bud, arching her back over his arm. A hot thrill shot through her, her breath caught, and all she could do was grip his arms and enjoy.

They burst into feverish motion again. Jack was trying to free her arms from her sweater as she attacked his shirt buttons, but they had to slow down, untangle with laughter, and unbutton each of his cuffs. With shirt and sweater finally flung aside, he crushed her close into a powerful, breathless kiss. The heat of his bare chest and arms and the hard press of his arousal were deeply soothing and intensely captivating.

As she greedily ran her hands over him, Jack deftly stripped her of the bra, baring her breasts to his intense gaze.

Her body simmered all the more under his steady scrutiny and hungry smile, and she was glad for the room's cool air whispering over her flushed skin. How could a look be both so adoring and so scorching?

"Damn, Cami, you are so beautiful." Then he scooped her into more lovely steamy kisses that erased every sane thought. He showered her with delicious torment, rough sensual massages of her breasts, reverent strokes of thumbs and palms over her nipples, and again and again the wet suckling warmth of his mouth tasting her everywhere.

Sinking her fingers into his thick hair, she pressed her body into his, wanting more and more as he turned her into liquid heat.

~*~

Sanity was overrated, right?

Jack couldn't get enough of Cami with his hands and mouth. She filled his senses, all soft and satiny, sweet and salty, warm vanilla and spice and the wine they'd shared.

She cupped her hand over his erection, her firm stroke electrifying his body and blanking his mind. He dragged in a harsh gasp. He needed her hand around him without a denim barrier.

Moving again as one between urgent kisses and seeking hands, tripping, and stumbling, they toed off shoes and socks, and wrestled with snaps, zippers, and tangled pants. Straining and riding together, he needed her wrapped around him, needed to get ever closer.

Still locked in the crazy, mind-gelling kisses, their hands touching everywhere, all he could think of was Cami and the yearning of the past six years. After so many mistakes, he'd finally found where he was meant to be. Every frustration, every jealousy, every pent desire broke free in a tidal wave of need, and every intelligent impulse drowned a happy demise under overwhelming elation.

They tumbled naked onto her sofa, Cami straddling him, pulling them together with a sweetly aggressive purr. She rode her center sleekly over him, hot and wet, and they shuddered together. She arched, lifting, driving down. "Jack, yes!"

He filled her, the pleasure an overwhelming, mind-blanking relief, and he surrendered, completely consumed in the hot, tight clasp of her, meeting her in the untamed pace she set, pumping hard and fast, overcome with the *yes, this now, hers, mine, us.*

A shred of regret whispered at racing through this first time together, but evaporated under the triumphant burst of finally, finally, Cami was his completely. At last, all was right in his world.

"Jack, there, more. Oh, you feel so good."

Delight shone in her face. She shifted, fingers biting into his shoulders, her muscles tightening, the roll of her hips sharper, her gaze locked on him, her plump lower lip caught between her teeth. Trembles ran through her, and her eyes glazed and darkened as her focus turned inward and sweet little cries laced her panting breath.

There was something he needed to remember . . . a vague idea to hold off, slow down zinged through his brain as he balanced between the pleasure/pain, and was as quickly abandoned as the need for release knotted in his belly and consumed his being.

"Jack! Yes, yes, yes!" On a strangled cry, her climax rocked her hard.

Rocked him, too. Feeling her tumble into ecstasy finished him. "Aw, now, honey, now."

He gripped her hips, plunging onwards with rough, greedy strokes, flying on the rushing bursts of incredible pleasure.

Panting and gasping, he collapsed over her, sweating and completely wrung out, floating on happiness. Yes, he could stay like this forever with Cami in his arms.

Comprehension trickled in.

They were together. He was clasped deep in her perfect heat.

Bare.

Oh, *shit*! Chill guilt sliced through him, clearing his mind. Never, ever had he made this mistake. He'd just screwed up horribly with the last person he wanted to cause any worries.

The first jolt of Cami's own awareness of his

blunder shook her. Her eyes flew wide open and she clenched around him. "Jack?"

"Shit, Cami. I'm sorry."

After a long, awful silent pause, she surprised him. Rather than pushing away and separating herself from him, she sagged into his arms and held tight, burying her face against his neck.

She groaned. "My fault. I don't know what came over me. Well, you came over me." Another groan lightened into a nervous chuckle. "I totally, utterly lost my mind. That also has never ever happened before. All I could think of was *you*. Needing you."

As he wrapped his brain around his major omission, he stroked her head, combing fingers through her silky hair. His wallet holding the condom they'd forgotten lay an easy reach away. No excuse whatsoever. His responsibility.

"No, not your fault. I'm so sorry, Cami. I'm never irresponsible like this. *Never*."

She lifted her head and met his eyes, her expression worried, but free of anger. "I believe you. As I said, it's my fault, too. I was a very willing participant. Extremely willing."

He drew in a long breath. He had to ask. "Ah, are you on anything?"

Her resigned sigh gave him her answer before she spoke. "No." She rhythmically tapped her fingers on his arm and he realized she was counting. "In theory, we're okay."

In theory wasn't absolutely. Another twist of guilt wrenched Jack. He was relieved she was so calm, but shouldn't he be freaked out that they could be facing pregnancy? Instead, he was contemplating that ring in his top drawer. Had he subconsciously screwed up on purpose?

Cami shivered. "I'm getting cold here." She kissed him as she slipped free and rose, lovely and somber in the soft light.

More guilt slid through him.

She scooped up her sweater, clutching it to her as she scanned the living room strewn with clothing, and shrugged with an embarrassed smile. "We made a mess and, oh, I'm so, so glad the drapes were closed." She held out her hand to him. "Let's go to my bed, it's more comfortable and warm."

They gathered the scattered clothes, and he followed her upstairs.

"I'll be right there." She ducked into the bathroom.

Still reeling under the combination of shock, guilt, and undeniably smug joy, he turned down the bedding and stacked the decorative pillows on the chair. He hadn't come over here tonight intending to end up in Cami's bed. Yes, maybe he'd hoped for a little fooling around and kissing before he headed home, but he hadn't expected their kisses to explode out of control.

Making love with Cami tonight had been crazy and unforgettable, but also more profound than simple sex. Truth was, while he'd been dreaming of this for six years, making love with Cami in reality far exceeded the best of his dreams.

When she rejoined him, he folded her into his arms and snuggled her close in the cozy bed, wishing he could find the right words to ease the quiet settling between them.

"Do you want kids?" He figured she did, but better to be clear and make sure they were on the same page. Better to discuss stuff late than never.

"Yes. Always have." She lifted away slightly, studying him with a pensive gaze. "How about you?"

"I do. I've always figured I'd have family someday. Only, I just never met the right woman."

Or had he been just waiting for the right one to finally be free?

"Really?" Her eyes narrowed.

He cupped her face, trying to fill his answer with the truth of his feelings. "Really. So, if my mistake tonight leads to a child with you, the baby wouldn't be a mistake, but wanted. I'd be happy. Okay?"

"I really think we're safe, but thank you."

"You're important to me, Cami. Tonight was special, and that's not just a line. I wouldn't hurt you for the world." He kissed her forehead.

"You're important to me, too." Her doubtful expression softened into a fragile smile.

He stroked her back, savoring the fit of her warm, naked body against his, and he hardened, his eager body blissfully oblivious to the serious moment they had going on here.

Now that he'd made it into her bed, he would do whatever it took to keep Cami in his life. He rolled her under him, and kissed her deep and slow, trying to convey reassurance and erase that worry from her eyes.

Time to start getting it right.

Chapter Seven

*C*AMI'S HEAD STILL SPUN IN EQUAL PARTS SHOCK and amazement.

"Tell me what you're thinking." Worry furrowed Jack's face as he braced over her on his elbows. He gave a gentle nip to her mouth.

Spill all that she was thinking? Oh, no, not going there, but she wasn't in the least angry with him. She was very equally at fault. In theory, by counting days, they should be okay, but that was far from foolproof.

Oh, and how wonderfully, terribly foolish they'd been. Excepting the accidental lack of responsibility, this night had absolutely exceeded her fantasies of how they might be together in incredible ways.

"That I'm okay." She stroked her fingers through his hair and pressed a kiss to his mouth.

However, what concerned her more at the

moment than a possible accidental pregnancy was the small, totally insane part of her chirping in optimism. She should be completely panicked, but that irrepressible hunger for her own child seethed with greedy hope. Crazy, a very risky way to start a relationship, or to gain her family's approval, or meet her expectations for a carefully planned relationship.

Did Jack honestly mean his promise when he said he wanted a family? He sounded sincere. He was so good with Emily, a natural with all kids.

But . . . she'd had men make her promises before, promise her love, promise they'd always be together, promise her children . . . and they all broke those promises so easily. Brent's email break up note and move without notice was simply the latest in the line of baffling rejections.

Jack cupped her head, locking eyes with her. "I promise you that. No matter what, you'll be okay." He kissed her hard. "We're in this together."

She sucked in a long breath. Okay, maybe she was a fool, but she could wallow in panic, or seize the moment and relish the loveliness and potential of what they had between them.

"I believe you. Thank you. Yes." Cami cupped his face and kissed his mouth, pondering words to reassure him fully. "I want you here with me."

Truth, absolute truth, even if an alarmed *Oh, my, oh, my! What had they just done?* still squeaked along her nerves. This relationship with Jack was changing so fast, but nothing in her life had ever felt as right. She blushed. What a wild, wonderful ride and a crazy, unforgettable night.

Jack smiled as if she'd just promised him the

world. "I don't want to be anywhere else."

He brushed her hair back from her face. "This time we'll take things slow." He lifted away and removed the condom from his wallet. "This time is for you."

This loving was sweet and relaxed and quiet, filled with kisses and touches, leisurely exploration with lips and fingers, shared breaths, moans, and shivers.

Jack filled her senses, her body, and, yes, even if she was far from ready to accept the immensity of the changes between them, her heart.

He rose on his arms over her, looking into her eyes as she opened her legs and welcomed his steady press. So ready for him, she nearly fell apart at his deliberate, deep thrust.

Slow still ruled. Jack moved with gentle, controlled strokes, simultaneously pleasing and incredibly frustrating. Needy, so famished, she impatiently slipped her hand down, touching herself, shuddering, breath rushing as he watched.

Heat flared in his eyes. "Oh, yeah, I like that. So hot."

She smiled as he shifted for a better view. Between his strokes and her touch, she came fast and sharp.

He gasped. "You feel so good around me. Aw, Cami." He increased his pace. "Wrap your legs around me."

Their tempo settled back into long and steady, their eyes locked together, words unnecessary now. The tension building, the friction incredible as he took her to the brink again and again. His muscles flexed powerfully under her hands, rhythm shortening. He shifted, bracing himself, widening his stance, catching a hand on her knee, pressing her wider. The sensual strain spurred a fresh wave of luscious heat, and she met his next drive, tightening on him, as she writhed impatiently beneath him needing more, deeper. Her legs trembled.

"There, there, oh, there, Jack."

As her release tripped and crashed over her with sparks and beautiful burn, he crushed his mouth down on hers and joined her, his body surging and straining.

When she could focus again, Jack held her snugly, his chest heaving, and her body tingled with little shivery aftershocks.

"You okay?"

"Very okay." She brushed a kiss over his mouth, drained, melted, and contented. "Marvelously okay."

They lay cuddled and quiet, and drowsiness was winning the battle with her spinning thoughts.

Jack brushed kiss over her cheek. "I should go and let you sleep."

"Don't go. Stay until morning." She tightened her embrace. Oh, had that sounded too needy?

"I'd like that." The husky warmth in his voice settled her nerves.

"Thank you."

She'd barely shut her eyes, or so it felt, when the alarm clock rang far too soon.

Cami hit the off button and collapsed back against her pillow and Jack's big warm body. As contentment rippled through her, she stretched and slipped an arm over his waist.

Jack groaned. "It's dark. It can't be morning already."

"Afraid so."

"I don't wanna go to school." He wrapped himself around her, nuzzling her throat, roaming his fingers over her skin.

Cami laughed. "Me neither, but we're the teachers. We have no choice."

She would much rather stay in bed in the cozy dark with Jack, cuddling against the tempting, comfortable heat of him and the hard seeking press of his arousal.

"We have a little time, right?"

She adored the hoarse urgency in his voice. "A little. Enough."

He rolled away and, after sounds of fumbling at the nightstand and a crinkling tear, he rolled back, tugging her to him with a growling laugh.

Need swelled, ached, and scorched and she met him with a laugh of her own as they tumbled in bed. The morning's lovemaking was sweetly hot, totally rushed, and perfectly imperfect.

Left too winded and happy to care, she rained kisses over his face. "Good morning."

His grin was clear even in the dark room. "Great morning."

Unfortunately, the morning was also marching along whether they liked it or not, and that meant time to be responsible, finally, and get ready for work. After a mug of coffee and breakfast together, she kissed him and sent him home in the shadowy dark.

As she showered, comfortable aches reminded her of every delightful moment, sending her thoughts tumbling again between delight, shock, and sheer panic.

Oh, what had she done? She pressed a hand over her belly. Oh, she'd been so insanely irresponsible last night. Most likely she was fine, but the timing . . . still close enough for concern. Oh, boy—and she'd thought just explaining that she was dating Jack would be difficult? What if she had to tell her family she'd also lost her mind, had been totally reckless, and was pregnant too? She winced.

Their spontaneous combustion last night shouldn't be such a surprise. Hindsight was great for seeing everything building to their impulsive encounter.

An echo of the pleasure he'd given her shivered through her core. She'd never been so thoroughly, wonderfully overwhelmed.

She needed advice. Mikki would have answers, but . . . no, just no. Pat? No, she wasn't ready to admit her big slip up to another person. She'd just research online. The sooner she knew for certain, the sooner she could decide how to handle matters.

Okay. Enough fretting. Time to focus on the positives. Last night and this morning had been wonderful.

What if she really was in love?

Only . . . to hope this amazing feeling was love was absurd, right? How could something so immense happen so quickly? However, instead, she was filled with the sensation that they'd always been together. Here was the zing missing from her life, and every moment with Jack felt so right, so much like she'd always wanted love to feel, a missing puzzle piece snapping perfectly into place.

If only Mikki were less dubious of a man like Jack for her. On one hand, Mikki usually had good advice, but on the other hand, this was her life, her future, and she was the only one who could decide which man was right in her life. If this was real, her family would come around. But this was so soon after breaking up with Brent. Did she really know what she was doing?

She lifted her face to the spray. Okay, enough. Positive outlook now. She was happy. She might be in love. Everything would be just fine.

~*~

That evening after work, Jack and Ray headed over to Tony Wescott's house to watch the playoff game. Tony and Nadine had three tiny, fun, and very loud children, two girls and a boy, but as Ray and he walked in, the house was strangely peaceful.

Jack glanced at the tidy family room as they followed Tony to the kitchen. "Where are Nadine and the kids tonight?"

"Nadine's having a girls' night out with Katie doing wedding planning stuff, and the three rugrats are being spoiled with a sleepover at their grandparents'."

The guys were all in the kitchen, busily snacking and piling food on their plates: Brian, Kerr, and Hale, as well as the newcomer to their group, Matt Powell, Tony's sister-in-law's fiancé.

Tony grinned and jerked a thumb at Matt. "Now that we're all here—Matt can break his news."

Matt nodded with a beaming smile. "Katie and I set the date. December eighteenth."

Jack clapped a hand on Matt's shoulder. "Hey, that's great. Congrats."

"Congratulations." Hale shook Matt's hand. "Best wishes."

Kerr raised a brow. "Wait. *This* December?"

Brian handed beers off to Jack and Ray. "Wow, so soon?"

"Yes. The place Katie wanted had a cancellation, and my sister and niece will already be here for Christmas, so we decided to go for it. We're more than ready for this step, so why wait? Save the date, you're all invited."

Tony handed Jack a plate. "Hey, Jack, Nadine has a friend who's interested in meeting you. She's a physical therapist, smart and pretty cute, and is into kayaking and hiking. You up for an introduction?"

Caught off guard, Jack scrambled for a reply. "Thanks, Tony, but I'm kind of seeing someone."

Lame, so lame. He was positively, completely, head-over-heels involved with Cami.

Ray perked up and paused in building his sandwich. "Really? That's right, you had a date on Friday. Guess it went well. Who is she? Is it serious?"

Damn. He didn't need Ray's interest in his social life right now. "Early days, but, yeah, could be. Uh, she's a teacher."

But, oh, yes, very serious on his end. Even more so now with that possible complication hanging over their heads. Crazy how intensely he wanted to spill everything he felt about Cami to the world. However, he'd promised secrecy.

"At your school?"

"No, at another. Ah, friends introduced us." True enough.

"You should bring her to the Halloween party."

She'll definitely be there.

"I'll think about it."

That party was going to be awkward. Remembering they were "just" friends around Ray and Mikki was already a pain, and resisting putting his arm around her, kissing her, or simply touching her was a constant struggle.

Cami and he definitely needed to discuss an end date to this secrecy.

"Great. See if she'd like to come. Tell her the more the merrier. You know us." Ray laughed. "I'll tell Mikki and Cami to hold off fixing you up with anyone."

Jack choked on his beer. "Right. Thanks. Don't need any surprises." He already had enough happening in his life.

After the game, Jack planned heading straight on home and to his own bed. It was late, Cami knew he was out with the guys, and she wasn't expecting him to call or come over.

However, her bedroom light was on, and he craved her too much. He waited in the truck until Ray disappeared inside. Hoping she was awake, he caved and called.

"Jack? Hi. I thought you were out with Ray tonight." Her soft drowsy voice made him want to hold her close.

"Just got back. I saw your light on. Did I wake you? I just wanted to say hi and good night."

"No, I was reading. Did you have fun tonight?"

"Yeah, it's always a good time hanging out with the guys. A crazy game."

"Who won?"

"Yankees took it in the bottom of the ninth. They were killing us. What did you and Mikki end up doing?"

"We unpacked another box and watched *Sense and Sensibility*. Then she was tired, so I chased her upstairs to sleep. She's so uncomfortable."

"I know it's late, and you're probably tired . . ."

Desperate much?

"Would you like to come over?" The sweet husky turn of her voice had him aching for her.

"Yes."

"Then I'm not too tired. I'll meet you at the door."

His breath clouded in the frosty night air as he walked briskly next door, fallen leaves crunching loudly under his feet.

Cami opened the door to him, wrapped in her fluffy purple robe. "Wow, it got cold."

She met him in a kiss, both of them fumbling the door closed and locked.

He slid his hands inside her robe, but his chilled fingers met warm bare skin instead of pajamas. She gasped.

"Sorry about that."

Cami just laughed and pulled him close. "That sure woke me up. Now we need to get you upstairs and warm."

More sizzling kisses delayed their progress up the stairs, but raised quiet laughter. Between kisses, she helped him peel off his sweater and shirt. Boots, belt, jeans, and socks followed, and by the time he'd stripped Cami of her robe and fallen with her into the soft bed and into another consuming kiss he was plenty warm.

Kneeling before her, he drank in the sight of Cami so lovely and flushed in the soft lamplight and her smiling bedroom eyes, sensual and deep.

Strange how, every time he was in Cami's arms and bed, he felt like he'd come home. Aching for her, he was torn between prolonging their sexy play and needing to be inside her now.

While the view was perfect, the night was too chilly to stay uncovered. He stretched over her and dragged the covers up to wrap them in a cocoon of warmth. He kissed his way down her throat and lower to her breasts, drawing the sweet tip of one into his mouth and relishing her gasps and sighs.

As he loved her breasts with his mouth, he slid his hand lower to graze and tease between her legs. She was so lusciously wet and hot.

With a gasp she arched against him and laced her fingers into his hair, clasping his head. "Jack, please, oh, there. Oh, yes."

He groaned. "Aw, Cami, you feel so good."

He suckled her nipple, rolling and flicking his tongue over the firm bud. Gliding circles with his fingertips, he followed the lead of Cami's gasps and sighs and sharp catches of breath as she shivered under him, her hips rolling in time with his strokes.

Still stroking with his fingers, he tore his mouth away, looking up to see her face as she came. "Come on babe, let it go. You're so close. So beautiful."

She jolted, crying out breathy and sweet, eyes glazing and shutting in pleasure's strain. Her hand tightened, pulling in his hair.

He smiled and kissed her mouth.

"That—that was . . ." Happiness shone in her dreamy eyes.

"Beautiful."

"Better than beautiful."

He laughed.

"But I need more." She tugged him close and nipped kisses at his lips. "Much more."

"Whatever you want. Everything."

Everything. Yes, he wanted to give everything he had of himself. In loving Cami, he'd finally found the perfect challenge, and it was better than beautiful.

~*~

Cami woke to the pleasure of Jack's caress drifting over her belly and breast and the firm, inquiring nudge of his erection.

With a happy sigh, she shifted, arching her back and raising her leg to let him fill her. Spooned together, they found a steady, luxurious pace. His slow, thorough loving and a long, rolling climax left Cami boneless, breathless, and feeling utterly cherished.

Jack nuzzled her ear. "Good morning."

"It's a very, very good morning now." She twisted in his embrace to meet the warm press of his lips. Oh, she could get very used to this.

"Would you like breakfast? Coffee?"

"I'd love some."

"I'm in the mood for eggs, bacon, and toast. I'll cook. Sound good?"

"Sounds delicious." Yes, she could very much get used to this.

"Plans for today?" He kissed her and slipped from bed.

"It's a normal Wednesday at school. We do have an art project involving paint. Combining paint with six-year-olds is always interesting."

"Good luck." He pulled on his T-shirt and pajama bottoms.

"Thanks. After school, I'm helping Mikki with food shopping. How about you?"

"A couple exams. Otherwise a normal day." He leaned down and brushed a kiss over her mouth. "Okay, I'll meet you down in the kitchen. Coffee and breakfast coming up."

After breakfast, both of them dragged their feet against that last morning kiss goodbye, as if it would be forever before they saw each other again instead of hours.

This became their routine for the rest of the week. Every night, after an evening of pretending they were still just friends around Mikki and Ray and then heading home alone, Jack would arrive at her kitchen door a short time later, and she would launch into his arms, every worry abandoned until morning.

Saturday dawned beautiful, sunny, and cold for their pumpkin picking trip. The extra hours before collecting Emily at nine felt like a gift and they indulged in a lazy, loving morning with breakfast in bed.

Emily laughed and squealed at most of the hayride decorations scattered along the tractor's route, eyes glowing with excitement and cheeks rosy from the frosty air. Jack did a great job diverting Emily's attention from the scarier displays and used the excuse of the bumpy ride to keep his arm around Cami's waist.

A free sugar pumpkin came with their hayride ticket, so the hayride ended at the pick-your-own pumpkin field where hundreds of small sugar pumpkins dotted the field on one side, and larger variety pumpkins scattered the other.

Jack pointed to the pumpkin by his foot. "Emily, look, here's the size you can take home. Find a good one."

"Okay!" Emily raced off, darting from pumpkin to pumpkin.

As they kept an eye on Emily, and Cami snapped pictures, Jack slid his arm around Cami, caressing a hand over her rear, teasing her with snatched kisses and nips at her ear. With Emily so focused on the pumpkins, Cami let herself relax, and she snuggled into him, enjoying his playful attention.

"Aunt Cami! Unca Jack! Look at my pumpkin. Look! Look!"

Both of them jolted, abruptly reminded they weren't alone.

Emily offered up the cute sugar pumpkin, grinning ear to ear.

Cami snapped her picture. "Looks perfect to me, sweetie."

"Where's your pumpkins?" Emily wrinkled her nose at their empty hands.

"We've been looking, just haven't found the right ones yet."

"I'll help! I know how!" Emily shoved the pumpkin into Jack's hands and bounced off, checking pumpkin after pumpkin.

After an excited hop and squeal, Emily raced back and raised up an oddly-shaped pumpkin.

"Got it. A hugging pumpkin, Aunt Cami. Just like you and Unca Jack." She handed off the pumpkin to Cami. "Now Mommy's and Daddy's." She raced away.

"Emily caught us hugging." Had she caught

their kisses? She couldn't tell Emily not to say anything. That might make it worse.

"Don't worry about it, Cami. We've hugged in front of her before."

He caught the pumpkin out of her hands. The deformed pumpkin did look like one half was hugging the other half.

"This could make a real fun jack-o-lantern."

Emily found two more pumpkins, and they loaded all the pumpkins into sacks.

Next, they took a picture of Emily sitting on a massive pumpkin easily three times her size. On the way to checkout, Emily spotted the mini gourds and wanted two for the babies so they could make a pumpkin family.

After the corn maze, they headed for the petting barn. Emily was in seventh heaven at seeing all the animals, but the other rambunctious children who were running about the barn kept her wedged in the safety of Jack's legs. Finally, she bravely petted a patient goat.

"Hey, Emily, look at that." Jack pointed to a sleepy ewe nestled in the wood shavings.

Cami laughed. A hen was roosting on top of the sheep and held tight even as a second hen tried to barge in on her wooly nest.

Emily wiggled and chattered as they waited in the pony ride line. She might have been shy in the petting barn, but once Jack lifted her into the saddle, Emily perched on the small, barrel-bellied pony like she'd been riding forever.

Cami snapped pictures as the handler led the pony on its plodding route around the corral while Jack waited for Emily at the dismounting stop.

Emily threw her arms around Jack. "Again! Again!"

The handler grinned. "Such a good little girl you have. You must be very proud parents."

Both caught by surprise, Cami scrambled her answer together first, "She's our niece, but yes, we're very proud of her."

They bought cups of hot apple cider, hot dogs, French fries, and apple cider donuts for lunch at the picnic tables, and an apple pie to take home to Mikki and Ray. Emily chattered nonstop through lunch and most of the ride home, until she fell asleep in her car seat for the last couple miles. She slept through Jack carrying her inside and Cami peeling her out of jacket and boots.

"Hey, sleepy lovey." Mikki kissed Emily's forehead. "Did she have fun?"

Cami grinned. "She had a fantastic time, and we took a million pictures for you. Want me to tuck her in upstairs?"

"Thanks. Then tell me all about it and show me the pictures. Oh, I wish I could have gone! Thank you two so much for taking her."

While Jack hooked up the camera to the television for the slide show, Cami slipped onto the sofa besides Mikki. "How are you feeling?"

Mikki rubbed her belly. "So ready for the girls to make their appearance. I want to see my feet again. I want my little sweeties to stop crushing my bladder and squishing my lungs. I want to hug Ray and have my arms reach around him."

When Emily came down from her nap, she launched into telling Mikki about her day, and she wanted to see all the pictures again and announced she wanted a pony for the backyard.

Once Ray arrived home, they went out on the deck to carve the pumpkins.

Emily patted the pumpkins. "Pumpkin for me. Pumpkin for Mommy. Pumpkin for Daddy. Baby pumpkins for Christie and Kaylie. Hugging pumpkins for Uncle Jack and Aunt Cami. I picked it special."

Ray laughed. "That one's so ugly, it's kind of cute."

Cami relaxed slightly, relieved that Emily hadn't explained just why she picked it special.

So many times that evening through finishing the Halloween decorations and making supper, she caught herself reaching for Jack, wanting to slip her arm around him, or hold his hand. Being lovers by night, but merely friends during the day was wearying and frustrating.

She took a tense breath. Time to deal. Her own fault. She'd set the rules.

She was mostly sure all was well, but she needed to stop her stress-inflating avoidance of the past few days and determine how soon she could confirm or eliminate the worry hanging over their heads.

Pat was right. Living with regrets would be worse than trying and failing.

She wanted to believe that this thing between Jack and her was love. Time to let go of her fears.

Chapter Eight

⭐

THAT EVENING, AS THE LIGHTS CAME ON IN Cami's place, Jack paused on his front step. He was already tired of this secret keeping. He sighed and let himself inside.

After gathering the grading he needed to finish into his briefcase, he tossed his toothbrush and things into a gym bag.

He doubted Ray and Mikki would have a problem if Cami and he were open about wanting a serious relationship. He could appreciate Cami's point on keeping Mikki from extra worries, but really, the point was moot. Unlike Brent and the other men who hadn't appreciated Cami, he wasn't going to jerk her around.

True, that they'd had gotten so close, so fast, might hit everyone as a surprise, but really, serious was a good thing, right? Anyhow, Ray and Mikki had gotten serious fast when they'd first met and, technically, since Cami and he had been friends for years now, this relationship wasn't even close to fast. As for Cami's parents, they liked him. He liked them. Everything should be good.

After a last check for anything he might need over at Cami's, he slung the bag over his shoulder, grabbed his briefcase, and then paused, studying his room.

He liked his home. The renovations had taken years, but he'd thoroughly rehabbed the formerly-trashed, neglected foreclosure from basement to roof. He could see Cami living here just fine. Her furniture would mix in well with his, and her great bed would be a perfect fit in his bedroom.

He crossed the hall to the spare bedroom's doorway. Empty but for a twin bed, nightstand, and lamp, the rarely used room was a blank slate ready to be transformed into a kid's room.

His gut took an excited, anxious swoop. If Cami was pregnant . . .

Stop. Everything's fine. Either way, you're making this work.

Cami greeted him at her kitchen door with a sizzling kiss that wiped all his concerns and the annoyances of their arrangement from his mind.

Dropping his bags on the kitchen table, he scooped her into his arms and carried her upstairs.

After a hurried stripping of clothes, they tumbled into bed, all hungry and crazy kisses and hands like their first time, except this time he remembered his responsibility.

Making love to Cami only got better.

Jack gripped her waist, pleasure roaring through

him, trying to slow down and savor the arousing sight of her sitting above him as he moved in her tight warmth, those brown eyes of hers wide and dark, her panting breaths, her shining fall of blonde hair dancing over full breasts, her nipples perfect, deep rose points.

His hands tightened, and he swallowed hard against the need to blurt his love. His voice cracked roughly. "You're so beautiful."

Delight sparkled in her smile. "Come kiss me." Cami leaned forward, bracing on her hands, silky hair spilling around him.

He seized her mouth, their tongues mirroring the slide and rush of their bodies together. He filled his hands with her breasts, the soft weight perfect, as if made for him. As he stroked his fingers over her nipples, she moaned sweet and low, her eyes falling dreamily half-closed, her body rising and driving down to meet him, rippling around him.

"Oh, oh, Jack. So good." Her head fell back and her rhythm grew sharp and urgent. Seeing and feeling her so close to coming excited the hell out of him. Slowing down and holding back were no longer options.

He stopped thinking and just let himself go, let it all flow through him: her warmth, the light floral scent of her soap and apple tea and their mingling sweat, their rough breaths and strained cries. He let go, and watched pleasure rock her. He let go, driving into his own release, and was swallowed, consumed, drained, and when Cami fell into his arms, all that was left of him was a deep swell of peace.

Jack woke to the steady patter of rain against the

window and the warm press of Cami sleeping beside him. Content, he lay quietly, watching her and savoring his good fortune, fully certain he hadn't been happier in his life.

After Cami woke, he headed down to the kitchen to fix their coffees and retrieve his gym bag. His head buzzed happily with ways they could enjoy spending the dark, rainy Sunday in bed, but a quiet coffee together was a pleasant beginning.

Today would also be a good time to begin talking about the future. He felt as if they'd been together forever and should already be discussing permanent kinds of things, like her moving in with him and marrying him. Yes, he was ready and certain, but she needed to be certain as well, and they needed to be on the same page. As for the keeping things quiet in public, that came with its own set of complications. He wanted to drop this just-friends lie and let the world know how awesome he felt about being in love with Cami.

Returning upstairs with their coffees, he handed off Cami's mug and settled into bed beside her.

She sipped at her coffee and smiled. "Thanks."

"You're welcome." He smoothed a lock of hair behind her ear and searched her beautiful brown eyes. Was the happiness he saw there also the love he believed they shared? They could make this work.

Time to trust, time to talk, no matter the awkwardness. This all churned in his gut. But where to begin?

He jumped straight in. "So, how long do we go on with this secrecy thing?"

Cami winced.

"And what happens if we slip up and someone catches on? That was a close call yesterday with Emily. Then there's the bigger issue of what if you're pregnant? The longer we wait will only make everything harder to explain."

Her breath caught. He'd wrecked their peaceful mood, and her somber, pained face made his heart ache. Clearly questions she was still unready to answer.

Not that he had any easy fix-all answers either.

He stroked her shoulder and arm and curled his hand around hers. "I don't want us to be a secret anymore. Being with you is the best thing in my life. I want to be with you without rules and worries. This sneaking around feels wrong, like we're doing something to be ashamed of, like you don't want to be with me."

Alarm widened her eyes, and she clenched his hand. "I do want to be with you. I want you here."

"But we need to decide what we're doing. I don't want you stressing over something that's not a real problem. I want us to agree on an end date to this secrecy. I want you to feel comfortable coming over to my place. I want to be free to kiss you and hold you whenever I want, without worrying who's going to see us, or what they'll think. I want to show everyone how I feel about you."

He could see her worry wheels spinning and racing. *Please, trust me here, Cami.*

After a long pause and a shoulder-squaring shiver, she met his eyes. "Okay, Halloween. We should know by then about, well, a baby or not. Then, no more secret."

He released his pent breath. One week from

today. Sooner than he'd expected. Much better. "Okay, I can accept that. But if we slip up before then?"

"Then I deal with it." She glanced away, her voice small and strained.

He cupped her face in his hand, gently making her face him. "*We* deal with it."

"Right. We."

~*~

Cami's agreement weighed on her mind all through the busy week.

On top of a lack of sleep due to flip-flopping nerves, not to mention Jack and she having been insatiable for each other despite the worries and nerves, today had been hectic with the school's adorable Halloween Parade and her class party. She'd never been so tired, or so glad to reach home on a Friday.

Her usual class moms had been unavailable, and she'd had four very nice, but all-thumbs newbies to help with the craft project that should have been peel and stick, but ended up needing copious amounts of glue and patience. Her head still rang from all the noise of students wired on excitement and sugar.

Oh, well. The kids went home happy, that's all that mattered in the end.

After changing out of her fairy princess costume into a soft T-shirt and her comfy fleece set, she poured a glass of wine, ready to head over to Mikki.

She froze, staring at the wine in her hand. What if she *was* pregnant?

No, she was okay. Think positive. Her period should be happening any hour now. She sucked in a hard breath and sipped at the wine.

Oh, who was she kidding? She had worries galore. This maybe baby changed everything.

She took another sip of wine. She could not panic. No panicking allowed.

If only she could talk to Mikki. But by her own rules, she couldn't tell Mikki anything for at least two more days, and even then . . .

Oh, Mikki would have fits when she learned about this particular problem.

Focus. One issue at a time. What did Mikki do about wine? Relax. Think. You know this.

Cami's breath whooshed out. One glass, on occasion. Okay, for today, just this single glassful. Just in case.

Oh, no—but caffeine! How could she give up coffee too? She loved her coffee.

Breathe. Moderation and weaning off onto decaf. You've been wanting to decrease caffeine intake anyhow. You can do this.

Why was she panicking? She'd been through Mikki's two pregnancies and knew the drill. And once she'd broken the news to Mikki, and Mikki finished freaking out, Mikki would have all the answers to the questions Cami's spinning mind couldn't collect. Oh, Mom would freak out too, but when she calmed, she'd also be a font of knowledge and support. So, no need to panic.

But . . . but . . .

Buck up and calm down. Go over to see Mikki. Spending time with Mikki and Emily will distract you. There's laundry to do and cooking and party prep details and keeping Mikki off her feet.

She could do this. Only a couple more hours

and she would see Jack. That would help. A few more hours after that, they'd be alone together, and maybe they could talk more. Well, he'd likely just reiterate the need to get everything out into the open. How could he be so calm about all this when she kept spinning out of control?

Stop. You're fine. Everything's going to be okay.

Cami headed for the breezeway. After one more pause to collect herself, she knocked at Mikki's kitchen door and opened it a crack. "Hello!"

"Hey, Cami. TGIF?" Mikki called out from the living room.

"Very." She found Mikki standing and folding a basket of freshly laundered clothes. "Mikki! You were supposed to wait for me."

Mikki clutched one of Emily's tops and sheepishly winced. "I know, but I was so bored and sick of sitting."

"You're just lucky I caught you and not Ray."

"I know. He'd throw a fit, but I've been lying around all day except to go to the bathroom and eat. I'm just antsy and fussing and so ready to deliver and so sick of being huge and fat and I've hardly had any sleep!" Her face crumpled and tears spilled. "And I don't know why we decided to hold this party with my due date coming up smack dab against it. What was I thinking? What if I go into labor during the party?" More tears flowed.

Cami handed her a tissue and hugged her. "Then let's cancel the party. Everyone will understand."

"But I want the party!" Mikki wailed.

"Okay, then it's simple. If you go into labor, we'll just move the party to the hospital. I bet the nurses would enjoy the antipasto tray, hot wings, and the pies."

That broke a smile out of Mikki, and she half-laughed, half-sobbed.

"Okay, scoot, sis, back on the couch." She guided Mikki into walking. "I've got the laundry. Why don't you work on the candy bags?"

Calmly managing Mikki's problems was so much easier than dealing with her own.

Mikki scrubbed palms over her wet cheeks. "Good idea. And Emily can help when she wakes up from her nap. She's been whiney and out of sorts today like me and wouldn't sleep."

After Mikki planted herself on the sofa, Cami brought her all the supplies for the candy bags.

Cami set to prepping the ingredients for the chicken vegetable soup for supper and the chili for the party. Soon the soup was simmering, and she was folding the next dryer load in the living room.

"Hey, Cami?"

"Hmm?"

Mikki pinned her with a thoughtful look. "I need to ask. Is there a problem between you and Jack?"

Cami flinched. "No. Why would you ask?"

"I don't know. Ever since the move, you've both been acting odd, like you're almost avoiding each other. Did something happen? Does Ray need to talk to Jack?"

"No! Jack and I are fine. Honest."

Oops. She ducked her head against the scorching blush, focusing intently on folding a T-shirt. Apparently, they'd been a little too careful on the keeping quiet side. But, oh, my, they most certainly hadn't been avoiding each other.

Mikki squinted at her. "Okay. I guess it's just my whacked-out hormones then. I've been so tearful and silly and exhausted lately. But, you'd tell me if there were a problem, right? You and Jack have always been friends. I'd hate to see something wrong between you two and be unable to help."

"Of course. No worries here. We're great."

An overwhelming rush of emotions engulfed Cami. Great? Not even close.

Oh, Mikki, Jack and I are terrific together, and I can't believe how much I feel for him, and I'm so scared we might accidentally be parents, because we totally lost our minds one night, but I need you and the babies okay before I can start sorting myself out and get this weight off my chest and ask for your advice!

Luckily, before she could explode and confess all, Ray and Jack walked in the door.

At Ray's wrapping Mikki in a gentle hug, with a kiss and rub to her belly, jealousy shot hard and sharp through Cami. She couldn't even glance at Jack for fear she'd give her feelings away.

Your own fault, you know. You made the rules.

The look in his eyes and a stolen kiss in the kitchen radiated his own frustrations.

Two more days, then she could toss her rules and her worries.

Toss your worries? Really? What if there is a baby? What if everyone is against you being with Jack?

During the hearty supper of soup and biscuits, Cami made a particular effort to chat normally with Jack about their day.

The World Series game had an eight p.m. start,

so after supper they all watched *Finding Nemo* until Emily fell asleep, and Mikki announced she was done in for the day. Cami helped Mikki put Emily to bed and joined the guys downstairs, but she couldn't relax enough to enjoy the game.

Maybe she was just a little behind, but feeling more like that time of the month was coming on would be nice. While she was generally very regular, she wasn't always perfectly on the dot and stress could delay things. A new school year, moving, and diving blindly into a relationship definitely counted as big stressors.

Stop, stop, stop! Worrying over something you can't have an answer to for several more days is ridiculous. You're either pregnant or you aren't. Today, you're fine.

Only, all these years of wishing and wanting and her rigorously repressed jealousy of Mikki's motherhood might be at an end—

But, this was so not how she'd envisioned welcoming a baby into her life. How had she so utterly lost her mind that night? Jack totally should be the wrong man but, when she was in his arms everything felt so right.

And she needed his arms now, but while they were here in Mikki's and Ray's house, she couldn't turn to him because of her own stupid rules.

At the prick of tears, she stood and collected her water glass. "Guys, sorry, I'm beat. Enjoy the game, and I'll see you tomorrow."

She added her glass to the dishwasher, started the wash cycle, and escaped to her apartment.

How could you want something so fiercely and at the same time be so terrified that your deepest wish might finally be coming true? This was going to complicate her life—*was* complicating her life. Moreover, if she was pregnant, how could she ever be sure of Jack's feelings—what if he didn't mean his promises? She'd had promises before—

Stop! Deep breath. Calm down. Focus on the positives. You know Jack. Trust what you know. Trust what you feel for him. On the plus side, if it's true, you should at least be able to finish out the school year.

But would she be able to teach in the fall? She'd always been careful with her finances, but could they afford to live without her income? Oh, she and Jack had so much to discuss. She'd always planned that she and the father of her children would sort these things out *before* starting a baby, not after.

Shakes rattled through her. She might be a mother in July. *This July!*

She crumpled in tears, fear and happiness too tangled together to sort out which the tears belonged to.

Come on. Snap out of it. Pull yourself together. Jack will be here soon, and you don't need him to catch you crying over what is almost certainly a non-issue. Today, you're fine.

She scrubbed her palms over her eyes. If she tossed her rules and talked to Mikki or Mom, would these crazy mood swings be eased?

Probably, but that was out of the question for now. Mikki needed to focus on only herself. As for Mom? Mom would help, but Mom also would tell Dad, and Dad would . . .

Oh, that was a conversation she dreaded.

Anyhow, the crazy mood swings were probably just PMS setting in. She fumbled a tissue out of the box, dried her eyes, and blew her nose. Time to stop emoting, stop avoiding, stop waiting on pins and needles for her period, and go online to research how soon she could get definite answer. Basic research for basic answers—that she could handle. No different than, say . . . learning what armadillos eat or how long an eaglet takes to fledge. Simple.

Okay, so stand up, go to the bathroom and wash your face. Then, turn on the computer and do what you know you need to do.

~*~

Jack forced himself to hang out with Ray until the sixth inning before he succumbed to the grinding need to follow Cami. She'd been distant and distracted all evening, and the cause was more than a long, hectic day at school. What if she was having second thoughts? He needed to be with her, not pretending interest in the game.

"Sorry, Ray, I need to crash. Long week."

"No problem. See you tomorrow."

As he packed his bag at home, he paused with his top bureau drawer open, tempted to take the ring with him.

Guilt rolled through him again. Despite his agreement to wait until Sunday, he'd deliberately risked getting caught kissing her in the kitchen. He was sick and tired of hiding their relationship. Would proposing now reassure Cami that he was sincere? Or would he only scare her away? Their relationship was the weirdest thing. Part of him felt they'd been a couple forever, but part of him warned against popping the question too soon.

When Cami met him at the kitchen door, she'd washed up and readied for bed, but scrubbing her face had failed to soothe the signs of crying. Her eyes were too bright, puffy, and reddened.

Was she going to back down on her promise to end the secrecy? How did he convince her she didn't have to worry, that he was fully onboard with her in this? This wasn't exactly a situation he'd needed to handle before in his life.

Maybe some tea would help. Cami and Mikki liked to sit down and chat over a cup of tea.

He brushed a kiss over her mouth. "Can we have some tea? Then sit in the living room and talk?"

"Okay."

While Cami readied the teakettle and mugs, Jack raided her cookie jar and piled a large handful on a plate. He set the plate and two napkins in the living room and headed upstairs with his bag. He kicked off his shoes and dropped his phone, watch, and wallet on the nightstand before heading back downstairs. Hedging matters? You bet. Stopping first in the living room, he scanned through her music CD's and selected a relaxing instrumental.

When he returned to the kitchen, the water was just beginning to hiss and rattle in the kettle, and Cami was standing at the sink, head hanging and hands gripping the lip of the counter.

Without a word, he wrapped his arms around her. She softened into his embrace with a sigh, and they waited like that until the water boiled. He went with the apple cinnamon again, and she chose mint.

They sat at opposite ends of her sofa. He'd rather hold her, but this was better for staying focused on talking.

He handed her a cookie and took a bite out of his. "So, no news?"

She bit her lip and shook her head.

"Either way, it's going to be okay, Cami. I promise."

"Just there's so much to think about." She dunked her teabag several times, but set the tea aside untasted.

"Yes, there is." He couldn't deny that. A lot to consider, a lot to plan, and a lot of explanations they'd be making either way. "But it doesn't need to be all thought out and decided at once. One step at a time."

"I'm not even technically late yet."

"Okay."

"I'm generally very regular, but glitches happen, and this has been a stressful fall. That can affect things."

"Understandable."

"You're so calm about this. How can you be so calm?"

"Have a bite of cookie and drink some tea." He ate another cookie and delayed answering her until she complied.

He locked eyes on her and pushed all of his conviction into his words. "Because either way, we'll be okay. Because either way, I love you."

Cami jolted, her eyes flying wide.

"Yeah. Hit me hard too. I'll say it again—I'm in love with you, Cami. I think I've loved you since I first met you six years ago, but I was too busy trying to do the *right* thing to recognize the truth. So, whether there's a baby or not isn't going to change how I feel about you."

"You don't have to say this because I might be pregnant."

"No, I don't. I'm saying I love you because it's true." He reached over and wrapped her hand in his. "You're not in this alone. So, first step—how soon can we stop wondering and find out for certain?"

"Ah, maybe Sunday. I read it's better to test a few days after a missed period."

"Okay. So we do this on Sunday, before the party. That work for you?"

She swallowed hard. "Yes."

He tugged her into his arms, and she came willingly. "You've known me for six years, Cami. You can trust me."

"I'm just so afraid I'm going to wake up one of these days and see it all slipping away."

The plain hurt and fear in her face tore at him. "Oh, sweetheart, I'm not slipping away. I love you."

She flinched back, but he tucked her close.

Right, she still wasn't ready to accept that yet. He plowed on, his heart aching for her, wishing he could erase all her worries. "Yeah, maybe it took me a while to realize it, but it's been a long time building. We know each better than some married couples I know of do."

"I'm afraid of what if it doesn't work out." Her voice cracked.

Jack crushed down the primal urge to hunt down and punch out every guy in Cami's past who'd let her down and slipped away. "Then let's make this work. I believe we can. We belong together."

"How can you be so sure?"

"There are no guarantees about anything in life, but I'm willing to take the chance, willing to believe we have a future together. You're worth the risks to me. I need to know if you feel the same about me. Do you believe we have a relationship that's more than fun moments and mind-blowing sex? Do you want to have a future together? If you do, we can make this work."

"Yes, I do."

The rising confidence in her voice knocked a ton of stress off his shoulders. "Then everything will be okay."

They had more nitty-gritty details to tackle, but that should wait for daylight and when Cami was rested. She'd had a hectic day with the busy school activities, helping Mikki with housework and prepping for the party, and topping all that off with the wondering about a baby . . .

Time to lighten things.

He kissed her cheek and snuggled her close. "So, if there's a baby, he or she will need a name. Any ideas? I'm figuring Spawn and Dude are out. Nemo? Coral? Dori?"

Cami laughed and some of the sparkle returned to her eyes. "Oh, please!"

"So, if we have a boy, what are your thoughts?"

"I've always liked the name Ryan. Sean is nice too."

"Both good. How about girl names?"

"Easier. Mikki and Ray went through so many choices for their girls, I thought about ones I liked as well. Lily and Grace were my favorites.

"I like those too." He kissed her. "I love you, Cami. I promise you, our being together won't upset Ray and Mikki and your family. Yeah, if there's a baby, they'll be surprised, but they're good people, and they love you. My parents will be disappointed with me for not being more careful, but in the long run, they'll be happy. They've always liked you. You can count on me. No matter what, we'll make this work."

"Okay." She burrowed into his arms. "I hope you're right."

The doubt in her voice and her not saying *I love you* back started an uneasy churn in his gut. Why was she making something so simple so complicated?

Chapter Nine

WAKING UP SNUGGLED AGAINST JACK'S WARM back was a lovely way to start her day. Cami drew a long, slow breath and let Jack's declaration from last night sink in, riding the dizzying waves of terror and elation. He loved her. No more wishful wondering, but reality.

After a pillow-muffled murmur, Jack stretched and rolled over to meet her in a kiss. His stomach growled. "Want some coffee and breakfast?"

"Sounds good. I'm hungry." Despite the dark pre-dawn hour, both their stomachs apparently remained on a weekday schedule and didn't care it was Saturday.

He rose out of bed, letting a cool draft flood her warm cocoon of bedding, but giving her a lovely view of his naked backside as he turned on the lamp. "Brrr. The floor's cold."

"Getting close to turning on the heat time. I hope all this frosty weather we've been having isn't a sign of a long, cold winter."

"I know what you mean. I always try putting it off until November, but October nights always tempt me to give in early." He tugged on his T-shirt and pajama bottoms. "I should have grabbed my slippers when I packed." He felt around on the floor and retrieved his socks.

Cami eyed the chilly distance between her and her pajamas and robe hanging on the rocking chair.

Jack grinned and handed over her pajamas. "I'll hit the bathroom first and meet you downstairs."

She huddled in bed, putting off the inevitable chilly rising until the toilet flushed, and then threw on her pajamas and slippers.

After a quick freshening up in the bathroom, which confirmed her monthly remained missing, she found the coffee perking and Jack foraging through her fridge.

"Coffee's almost ready." He emerged with the carton of eggs and chunk of cheddar cheese and set them on the counter.

Cami answered the quiet question in his expression. "Still nothing."

She wrapped her arms around him, resting her head against his shoulder, emotions swelling, appreciating his solid, comforting presence. "I'm sorry I was so stressed out last night."

He rubbed her back. "Stress is reasonable. I'm so sorry I put you in this position. But, baby or not, I promise you, I'm not going anywhere. I'm yours for good."

Her niggling worries scrambled to pinpoint

some doubt in his vow, but he was all calm, concrete fact.

He skimmed his lips over her throat, the sensation completely distracting her from their discussion.

"Oh, that feels so good." She arched in his arms and slid her hands under his T-shirt, savoring the warm bare skin of his back beneath her hands and hard press of his arousal.

"Love your hands on me." He dragged his shirt over his head and tossed it aside to the table.

"I love the way you feel. I love the way you make me feel."

She sank into his kiss, the consuming need for him alight once more. Hadn't she decided it was time to trust her feelings? Being cautious had gotten her men like Brent. Being cautious hadn't protected her from pain.

In for a penny, in for a pound. Time to tell him she loved him too.

"Jack?"

"Hmm?" He cupped her bare breasts under her top, rolling his thumbs over her nipples.

Sweet pleasure zinged through her core and she gasped, utterly distracted.

"Let's go back upstairs," he murmured in her ear as he roamed his hands downwards to slide beneath her pajama bottoms, caressing her lower and lower. "I can wait on coffee if you can."

A kiss, and another, his naughty, questing fingers doing delicious things.

"What coffee?" She nipped at his lips, sighing as he opened his mouth hungrily to hers. She moaned in delight and clutched his shoulders as she rode his hand. Need blazed. Upstairs would take too long. She had a perfectly good kitchen counter.

"Oh, Jack, so good—"

The breezeway door slammed open. "Cami! I need you to watch Emily. Mikki's—" Ray skidded to a halt, his mouth dropping open. "What the hell!"

Cami froze. Caught, oh, very caught. Her brain spun, empty of explanations.

Jack shifted first, easing his hands from her pajama bottoms and stepping back. "Ah, Ray . . ."

"You son of a bitch!" Ray exploded into motion, flying across the kitchen to slam a fist into Jack's face.

Jack crashed back into the cabinet.

Ray slugged him again, driving a fist into his belly, doubling him over.

Cami leapt at Ray, clutching at his arm before he could hit Jack again. "Stop it! Stop it!"

Ray flicked her off, grabbed Jack, and threw him at the door. Jack hit hard and tumbled to the floor, gagging for breath.

Terrified and furious, Cami jumped between Ray and Jack, slamming her palms against Ray's chest. "Stop this! Are you nuts? Why did you hit him? Why did you barge in here? Get out! Get out!"

She shoved him again, and this time Ray stepped back, breathing hard, his face still brick red with rage.

Mikki's faint cry broke the silence. "Ray? What's going on? Ray!"

Sanity returned to Ray's eyes, and he dragged in a hard breath. "Mikki's in labor. We're going to the hospital. Emily's asleep. Watch her."

He bolted from the kitchen, slamming the

breezeway door behind him.

Cami dropped to her knees beside Jack. His eyes were shut. He hadn't moved. How hurt was he? Ray had hit him so hard.

"Jack, oh, Jack, I'm sorry. I'm so sorry. Please be okay. Please, open your eyes. Talk to me."

Jack gave a pained grunt and grimaced.

She cupped his face gently, alarmed by the blood at the corner of his mouth. She'd never had to deal with violence worse than small playground tussles before. What if Jack was really badly hurt?

"Jack, please, open your eyes."

Ice, she needed to get him some ice for his face. "I'm getting you some ice. I'll be right back."

She darted to the freezer. Ice cubes? No, the bag of frozen spinach would do for an ice pack. She wrapped the bag in a dishtowel and knelt beside Jack.

Ray and Mikki's minivan rushed down the driveway past her window.

She gingerly touched the bag to his cheek, scared that he still hadn't opened his eyes. Should she call 911?

Jack groaned. "Shit!"

She yanked the spinach away. "I'm sorry."

He opened his eyes, his face pinching, and caught her hand and the spinach back to his face.

"Where's Ray?" He spoke carefully, each movement of his mouth obviously painful.

"Taking Mikki to the hospital."

"She's in labor? Now?"

"Yes."

He shifted miserably, pressing a forearm over his stomach. "Damn."

"What can I get you? Oh, Jack, I'm so sorry. Should I call 911? What if you're really hurt? I think you were unconscious."

"No. Wasn't really out. Just need to lie here until my head stops swimming." He shivered.

"I'm getting you a blanket."

What if he was going into shock? She felt shocky herself, chilled and sick, and her ability to think clearly was all gummed up.

"Okay. Floor's cold."

She sprinted to the living room and grabbed the throw blanket and a sofa pillow.

As she tucked the blanket around him, he lifted his head gingerly for the pillow, looking more alert.

"How are you feeling?"

"Like a truck hit me. Ray has a fist like a rock. Damn."

That Ray could hurt his best friend was completely surreal. "I'm so sorry. I should have locked the door. I didn't think to lock the door. They always knock first. I'm sorry."

He gingerly moved his mouth, as if checking his teeth with his tongue. "Not your fault."

"How are your teeth?"

"All accounted for."

The breezeway door creaked open. "Mommy? Aunt Cami?"

Emily stood there in her fleece sleeper, dragging her blankie and doll. She stared wide-eyed at Jack. They couldn't joke away the smear of blood on his mouth.

"Unca Jack, why're you on the floor? You hurt your mouth?"

"I'm okay, sweetie. I just slipped and fell. Aunt

Cami is making me rest here with an ice pack until I feel better."

"Mommy says no running in socks. You'll slip." Emily padded over and poked at his sock-covered toes.

He chuckled painfully. "Mommy's right."

Emily draped her blankie over him, tucked her doll into the crook of his arm, and snuggled against him like a puppy. "Miss Tracie gave me an ice pack at school when I fell. Made it all better."

Cami wet a paper towel and cleaned the blood from his face. If only she could curl up and disappear or rewind time.

~*~

He should get up, Cami needed him, but even parts Ray hadn't hit hurt, and holding the icy bag against his face was all Jack could manage at the moment.

About ten minutes later, Jack patted Emily. "I'm going to sit up."

Emily scooted off the blanket, and Jack shoved himself up to sitting without his head spinning too badly, but he rested against the cabinet before attempting to stand. Ray had nailed him but good.

After accepting Cami's offered hand up, he tottered over to sit at the kitchen table. She handed him his T-shirt and he gingerly pulled it on, everything hurting as he moved.

"What can I get you?"

He gingerly felt over his swelling cheek and replaced the pack of spinach against his face. "I could use some aspirin."

Emily climbed into the chair beside him and offered him her doll. "Did Mommy and Daddy go to get the babies?"

Cami fished the aspirin out of her purse and shook out two tablets. "Yes, honey. I'm sorry you woke up alone. They just left, and I was coming right over. Daddy said you were sleeping."

Cold guilt churned in Jack's gut. Emily always slept like a log—except for today of all days.

Anger flared behind guilt. What the hell was wrong with Ray?

Cami handed him the tablets and a glass of water.

"Aunt Cami, I want to see the babies."

"They're almost here, but not quite. We'll see the babies as soon as Daddy calls and says they're ready."

"Aunt Cami, I'm hungry."

"Sure." She set a cup of coffee in front of Jack. "I'll make you a smiley pancake, how about that?"

The phone rang. As Cami talked to her mom, she pulled the apple juice and milk from the fridge and gathered the ingredients for pancakes. He only half-listened to their conversation and sipped at the coffee. His headed pounded too much to focus.

"Okay, see you then." She hung up and turned to Jack. "Mom and Dad are on their way down, and they're going to stop here first, and then we'll all head over."

Emily hopped off her chair and tugged on his shirt. "I hafta go potty," she announced solemnly and then trotted off into Cami's half-bath, shut the door, and began singing the ABC song.

He couldn't help smiling even though it hurt. He pushed up from the table. Dizzy, but manageable. "I'm going to get my stuff together and head home."

"Are you sure? Maybe you should just rest here awhile longer."

"I'm fine. I have a hard head. Your parents are coming. You need to feel free to head over to the hospital and not worry about me."

"That won't keep me from worrying. I don't know what got into Ray. I've never seen him so angry. Why on earth would he hit you? You're his best friend."

"Wish I knew."

Figured, after promising Cami that her family would be fine with them being together and that everything would be okay, something had to go haywire.

Being caught seriously making out in the kitchen when nobody knew they were together was obviously part of the reason, but, instead of natural shock, Ray had been beyond enraged.

Cami shook her head. "I'll try to talk to him when I get to the hospital."

Dressing and packing up was a slow motion effort. By the time he came back downstairs, Emily was at the table eating her pancake, and Cami was turning a new batch on the griddle.

"Do you want some?" She looked so sweetly worried; he just wanted to hold her.

The pancakes smelled good, but he couldn't face chewing anything at the moment.

"No, I'm good, thanks. I'll see you later."

The cat was out of the bag, so after patting Emily goodbye, he kissed Cami at the door and trudged home.

A hot shower eased up some of the aches and

pains, and he grabbed an ice pack from the freezer for his bruised face and blackening eye. That was going to look just great at school on Monday.

After making himself eat some oatmeal with a banana, he stretched out on the recliner with the papers he needed to grade, but between his anger with Ray, headache, and throbbing face, he couldn't focus enough to do his students' work justice.

He set the stack aside on the coffee table and dragged the throw blanket over him. If only Cami would call. No matter how he tried to wrap his brain around the problem, he couldn't see what had enraged Ray. Ray wasn't the kind of guy to flip out without a reason. This was not okay.

He woke to his doorbell ringing. He pried himself out of the recliner on the springing hope it was Cami. However, the shadowy figure through the pebbled glass of the front door was too tall and bulky for Cami or even Ray.

Puzzled, he opened the door.

Cami's dad stood arms crossed, and he scowled at Jack, looking a little too pleased with Jack's messed-up face.

Ah, shit. Jack sucked in a breath and opened the storm door. "Mr. Alexander, hello. Would you like to come in? How's Mikki?" He stepped back.

The usually mellow Mr. Alexander loomed liked a disgruntled bear into his foyer.

"Mikki and the babies are doing good, but it's going to be a long day. She left a bag at home, so I figured this would be a good time for you and me to have a little talk." He planted his fists casually on his hips, nailing Jack with a scathing stare.

Oh, hell. Ray had already talked to Mr.

Alexander? Secrets never were worth the trouble they caused.

"I've known you a long time now, son, and I'm real disappointed in you. Real disappointed. You're going to stay away from my daughter."

His hackles rose. No way in hell was he agreeing to that.

He squared his aching shoulders. "No, sir. That's not happening. Cami and I are dating. No one has a say in this matter but Cami."

Iron gray brows narrowed over hard brown eyes. "You're dating my daughter? *You?*"

"Yes."

Hell, how many barbecues and parties had they spent together over the years, and now Mr. Alexander was looking at him like he was shit under his shoe? What the hell had happened today? Maybe he was unconscious and this was just some bizarre dream.

"I'll repeat myself so it's clear. Stay away from Cami. Stay away from Mikki. I don't want to see you near either of my girls."

"No. Are you going to take a shot at me too? Ray did already. Don't know what the hell his problem was with me when he's the one who barged in on us without knocking."

Mr. Alexander barked out a harsh sarcastic laugh. "You don't? Seems clear to me you deserved it from what I've heard."

What the hell?

"I've done nothing wrong."

He wracked his brain, but everything was fine up to the moment Ray had stormed into the kitchen. The only possible issue that could account for such anger was the possible pregnancy, but he hadn't talked. Had Cami? No, she was dead set on keeping things quiet, so he trusted she would have warned him if the news had slipped out.

Why was he defending himself? Mr. Alexander's stony expression showed he couldn't care less what Jack said in his defense. They'd all gone nuts.

"You can't threaten or scare me off. Cami is too important to me. Hell, the full truth is I love Cami. I've loved her since we first met."

"You have a damned strange way of showing it. Stay the hell away from my daughter." Mr. Alexander wheeled about, shutting the door between them hard enough to rattle the pictures on the walls.

Jack shook his head and immediately regretted the impulsive movement.

Damn, his head hurt. He glanced at the clock. Almost noon. Close enough to time for more aspirin. He took two more tablets with a tall glass of water, and slumped onto the sofa. He stared at his cell phone, willing Cami to call soon with answers. If Mikki wasn't in labor, he'd corner Ray and shake out what the hell his problem was, because not one damned bit of what had happened this morning made sense.

~*~

Cami glanced at her watch. Noon. Maybe she could slip away to call Jack and see how he was feeling. Things were calm here. Mikki's labor was in the early stage. Ray's dad and mom had volunteered to take Emily over to the park to play and out to lunch.

Mom narrowed her eyes at Cami. "Are you feeling okay, honey?"

"Me? I'm fine."

Oh, Mom, if you only knew. I'm in so much trouble here.

Mikki duplicated Mom's narrow eyed stare. "Are you sure? You seem off."

"Totally fine."

"You're not worrying about me are you?" Mikki glanced up at the monitor. "You heard the doctor. Everything's going great. I'm fine. The girls are fine. Just playing the waiting game now. Ray's wound insanely tight though. I'm tired of kicking him out to chill down in the cafe with Dad. I kept telling him I'm okay. I could have stayed home this morning, but no, he made us run to the hospital before breakfast like crazy people and forgot my bag. We have hours and hours to go before the girls are ready to arrive."

Cami fought a wince. She'd been glad to avoid Ray after the disastrous morning. He'd muttered a curt hello and, besides surreptitious glares, that had been the extent of their interaction at the hospital.

"Sorry, I can't help worrying about you, Mikki. It's in the sister handbook, you know."

Too much was going on for one day. She wanted to stay with Mikki, she needed to be with Jack, she wanted to confront Ray, she needed to deal with her own personal problem.

Worse, what if Mom and Dad learned about this morning's chaos in the kitchen? She had no idea how to explain that mess or break the news of Jack and her as a couple, let alone the possibility of a baby.

Mikki laughed. "Cami, do me a favor, please? See if Ray's calm enough to come up. Then you and Mom can take a lunch break."

Cami firmed her smile over the flip of her stomach. "Sure." She had to face Ray at some point and set him straight on her feelings for Jack. Might as well be now.

A good plan, while it lasted. Instead, Dad and Ray cornered her in the coffee shop.

Dad glowered like a thundercloud. "We need to talk, Camille. I need to know if what Ray told me is accurate. You're dating Jack O'Malley?"

She turned on Ray. "How dare you go tattling! This is none of your business."

"You're family, and I look after family."

"You had no right to hit Jack!"

Dad shook his head, his face creased in a hurt frown. "I'm real disappointed in you, Camille. How long have you been carrying on together?"

"We haven't been carrying on. We've wanted to be with each other for six years, but were never free to do anything about it until recently. We started dating right after I moved into the apartment—"

A growl rumbled out of Dad. "You've been dating less than a month, and you're already sleeping with him?"

"When the hell have you been dating him?" Ray snarled.

Her face burned. "I don't have to justify myself to you, Ray. I can date whom I like. You had no business barging in on us without knocking. I can do as I please in my own home."

"Mikki was in labor, and I didn't exactly expect to find you with Jack's hands down—"

"Ray!" Her blushed flared to scorching. Bad enough Ray had seen that, he didn't need to tell Dad.

"I can't believe you and Jack together in the first place . . . You know what he's like."

"So what? We're adults. We can be together if we want. But you hit him! He's your best friend."

"I hit him because he's seeing someone else while messing around with you."

Cami froze. Seeing someone else? "Are you sure?"

"Hell, yeah, I'm sure. Jack even told me don't try to fix him up for the party because he was seeing someone."

A fierce pang struck, and she sank onto a chair. "Who?"

"Some colleague, I guess. He didn't mention her name. I told him to bring her to the party, but he sidestepped giving me a yes or no. Now I know why. The bastard."

"I don't believe he'd do that to me. I've known Jack for six years. If he's such a two-timing jerk, why did he wait until both of us were free to date?"

Dad fisted his hands on his hips. "Then why all the sneaking around? Seems like the actions of a guilty man to me. Why not just tell us you two were dating?"

Ray sneered. "Because he didn't want to get caught."

"*I* wanted it kept quiet, not Jack. *I* asked him to say nothing because Mikki was all worried about me breaking up with Brent. I didn't need her adding new worries over nothing."

She shoved out of her chair and whirled on Ray.

"And if Jack is such a jerk, why is he your best friend? And what kind of best friend are you to him if you punch him without letting him explain himself?"

Dad caught her hand, brown eyes stern. "You stay away from him, Cami. He's no good for you."

"I finally date a man I want, who makes me *happy*, and you both jump down my throat. I dated all those men who were what I thought you wanted for me. What good did it do me?"

"I've told him to stay away from you."

Told him? She yanked her hand away, and restraining the need to yell took all her resolve. "You've already talked to Jack? Without talking to me? When did you talk to him—oh, when you ran home for Mikki."

"The fact remains he lied to you. He's seeing someone else."

"I don't believe you. I won't believe you. Jack needs to tell me the truth to my face." She snatched up her purse. "If Mikki asks for me, tell her I'll be back later. And don't you dare worry her with any of this."

As she bolted for the door, Dad caught her arm. "Honey, don't go driving while you're upset."

"I need answers now. I can't believe you confronted him without talking to me first. I'm not happy with you or Ray right now."

She wrenched free and charged off, pulse speeding and head pounding, completely gutted. They had to be mistaken.

Dad was right, driving upset was a bad idea, but despite her shriveling, whirling emotions, she held it together on the short drive. Just whom did she trust?

Family who loved her? Or the man she'd fallen hard for?

Maybe made a baby with . . .

However, when she reached home, an unfamiliar sedan stood parked in Jack's driveway, glossy and new, with the paper registration in the rear window.

Her throat constricted. No, she wouldn't believe Ray and Dad were right. It was Saturday. Jack always had friends stopping by. She parked at the street and leadenly walked to Jack's door, fighting the urge to run home and hide away.

She rang Jack's doorbell. Company or not, Jack and she were dealing with this right now.

He opened the door. His poor face was already turning a painful rainbow of color. Wariness in his eyes flooded to happy relief. "Cami!"

Hope fluttered. Would he be that openly happy to see her after Dad's earlier visit if he was cheating? She ignored the urge to throw her arms around him. She had to know the truth.

She choked out her question. "Are you seeing someone else?"

"What?" He stared at her like she had two heads, and then his expression shifted, and he glanced uneasily inside to his living room.

Cami's heart plunged. Hating this, she barged past him, needing to know who was in his living room.

Angela sat cozily on the sofa, looking gorgeous and unruffled, holding a nearly empty glass of wine.

Gutted, Cami struggled for breath. "How could you?"

Chapter Ten

![starfish illustration]

*J*ACK GROANED. THE SHIT JUST WOULDN'T QUIT today. "Cami, let me explain." He caught her arm, stopping her from bolting for the door.

"Ah, this is my cue to leave." Angela set down her glass. "But first, Cami, this is not at all what you obviously think. Jack and I aren't back together."

"Then why are you here?" Cami pulled against Jack's grip, but he gently held firm.

Angela shook her head as she stood. "Not for any of the reasons you're thinking. Jack and I are friends. That's all. I needed his advice on my new car. And here's something you clearly need to know. I broke up with Jack because of you. It was so obvious to me how hung up you were on each other. The vibes just poured whenever you two were around each other. I couldn't compete. I'm just surprised figuring it out took you both so long. He's all yours, Cami, and I honestly want you both to be happy."

Cami stood silent, mouth agape.

Jack lifted his own mental jaw up off the floor, stunned that Angela, of all people, had picked up on the attraction to Cami he'd always fought to subdue.

Angela slipped on her coat and patted Jack's shoulder. "Thanks for the help. Now, my advice to you two is to sit down and talk to each other. I'll let myself out."

Icy, sinking despair gripped Jack. Judging by Cami's face, she doubted Angela's every word.

The door clicked closed, and they were alone.

Cami pinned hurt eyes on him, stiff and resistant under his hands. "If you aren't seeing her again, why was she here?"

"It's the truth, Cami. I told you Angela and I parted friends. Yes, the timing could have been a hell of a lot better, but she simply needed advice on her new car. We're friends. I don't turn away friends."

She nodded and sucked in her breath. "Okay. But I have to know. Are you seeing someone else?"

Where the hell did that idea come from?

"No! No, I'm not seeing anyone but you. Why would I want to? When the hell would I have time to? I'm either working or I'm with you or with Ray and Mikki. I don't understand where this is coming from."

"Ray told me you said you were seeing someone. He even invited you to bring her to the Halloween party."

After a sluggish moment of trying to process that, comprehension flared, and Jack burst out laughing. "Oh, that." The insanity of the day finally all made sense.

His relieved laughter probably wasn't the smartest response. Cami's eyes narrowed, and the hurt on her face deepened. "Oh, that? What does *that* mean? You are seeing someone?"

He stroked her arms. "What that means is your insistence on keeping quiet about us made me scramble for a story when Tony wanted to fix me up with a date in front of Ray. I didn't want Ray and Mikki springing a blind date for me on us at the Halloween party, and I couldn't tell Ray you were my date. So, as vaguely as I could, I explained I was seeing someone. Which is true—I'm seeing *you*."

"Oh." She stopped fighting his grip.

"Maybe I should have managed my dating life better in the past, and, yes, I've made some mistakes, but I've *never* cheated on any of my girlfriends. I want to be with you. Just you. You are the only woman in my life."

She crumpled in his embrace. "I'm sorry. I didn't want to believe Ray, but he was so furious with you, I thought it had to be true."

"We wouldn't have had this problem if we just were open about how we feel about each other. Keeping secrets always screws things up." He stroked her back, so relieved this mess was almost resolved. "What a crazy day. First Ray punches me, and then your dad threatens me. I was real confused."

"I'm so sorry. I should have trusted you."

"At least now Ray flipping out this morning makes more sense. Would have been nice if he'd asked questions before punching me, but you're a sister to him. He was furious with Brent, you know."

"He was?"

"Ray cares about you. He hated how Brent treated you."

"I'm sorry my family went nuts on you." She gently kissed his mouth. "Dad really threatened you?

"I've never seen your dad that angry before. He loves you. He was worried for you."

"I'm sorry I kept you a secret. That was unfair of me. It's my fault you were hurt."

"Could have been worse. Good news is we're no longer a secret, and we can do this whenever we want." He kissed her. "I want to tell everyone how I feel about you. When I said I love you last night, I meant it. You're the woman I love. You're the woman I want to spend the rest of my life with. You're the woman I want a family with."

"This has been so fast. How can you be sure so soon?"

"Not so fast. You've known me six years, and I've been falling for you for six years. You can ask me anything. I'll always tell you the truth."

Cami's long pause sparked a new round of worry.

Then she nodded, as if having made a decision. "Tell me about Janine. I overheard Ray say she broke your heart, and she's the reason you never get serious with anyone."

He sighed. "Let me pour you a glass of wine, and let's sit." A half-glass for him should be okay with the aspirin.

They settled facing each other on the couch.

He gathered himself together. "Maybe Janine was the reason years ago, when the breakup was still fresh and painful. She and I were never engaged, although we'd been dancing around the idea. We should never have stayed together as long as we did. We didn't know how to talk to each other, we didn't want the same things, and we had unrealistic expectations of each other. A bad setup for a lasting relationship, and we made each other miserable. As for a broken heart? Well, undeniably battered and bruised. My never getting serious after Janine was mainly because I'd learned getting serious with the wrong woman was useless. I made up my mind not to get involved with anyone unless I enjoyed being with them. The plan mostly worked. I met some nice women, had fun, made some friends, made some mistakes, and kept moving on. Then Ray met Mikki. Mikki was nice, but she didn't do anything for me beyond, yeah, she's beautiful, and I'm happy for Ray."

He leaned forward, resting elbows on knees, locking eyes with Cami.

"Then, I met you. Seeing you for the first time was a total rush, like the sun came out, and my simple plan got complicated. Worse, you had a boyfriend, Scott. Our timing stayed screwed up ever since. I never could get serious about anyone because there you were, reminding me what I really wanted. And, yes, there's been woman after woman, because I kept looking for what I felt for you in them, but none of those women ever came close."

Her expression warmed, filling with surprise. "I never knew."

"Because I worked hard to be a gentleman and a

friend, keep my hands off, and make sure to keep my mouth closed. Even though it killed me every time you brought those guys around."

"I never ever guessed. I'm sorry. Would you believe I thought the same? How many times I wished you'd just give me the tiniest hint you thought I could be more than a pal?"

"Figures." He chuckled and curled his hand around hers. "Maybe it was more than bad timing. Maybe we simply weren't ready. We can't fix what might have been, signals might have been crossed, but things are clear now, and we can go forward from here. I enjoy being with you, and more importantly, I love you. We're good together. I'm praying you feel the same."

"I don't want you saying this just because you think you need to do the honorable thing."

What could he do to eliminate that damned fear of hers? How could he prove he wasn't going to slip away?

"I'm not. This is how I feel about you. Baby or no baby, I love you."

~*~

Still raw from the day's emotional tumult, Cami scrutinized his face, but found only earnest warmth in his blue eyes, his expression all loving.

Admit it. Let this be real. Stop finding excuses.

"I love you too." She shuddered with the release of tension and met him in a hug.

"Then we can handle anything."

They simply held each other for a few minutes, her strain vanishing under the flood of peace.

He rubbed her back and kissed her. "Finish your wine, and then we'll head to the hospital. You need to be there for Mikki."

"Are you sure you want to come?" Jack and she may have resolved things, but Dad and Ray might not be so easy to soothe.

"Hey, no doubts now. Let's get everything out in the open. Give me a minute to wash up and get as presentable as I can, and we'll head over."

"Also, I—" she blurted.

No more stalling. Face this all head on. You can do it.

"I need to make a quick stop at the drugstore on the way. Not here, the one closer to the hospital." In town, running into someone she knew was all too easy. Only so much openness she could handle in one day.

He cupped her cheeks and nodded. "Okay."

All too soon, they were waiting at the light just before the drugstore.

"Still want to stop now? We can stop on the way home instead, if you want."

"No, let's do it now. I can't put this off."

He pulled into a parking spot near the entrance. "Want me to come in with you?"

"It's okay. I'll just be a minute."

With tension knotting her insides and her fingers crossed, she strode into the busy store. Please, please don't let me run into anyone I know. She hurried to the aisle and selected the brand Mikki had used, hand shaking as she picked up the box.

Tomorrow. She'd know for certain tomorrow. They'd both know.

Naturally, checkout had a young man for a cashier and a long line, but thankfully, they were all unfamiliar faces. Unable to meet his eyes, she grabbed the receipt, buried the bag in her purse, and hurried out to Jack. She sagged into the passenger seat, already exhausted, and she still had an uphill emotional conflict ahead.

Jack leaned over and kissed her quick and hard. "It's going to be okay."

"Right. Waiting might make it harder and worse. Doing this now is best. No one is going to want to make a scene in a hospital."

"Ray may be busy, but we can at least square things with your dad."

Cami twined her hand in Jack's as they entered the hospital. This couldn't be a more awkward time to sort things out with her family. Her heart remained lodged in her throat all the way to Mikki's room and as she poked her head in the doorway. Just Mom, Dad, and Ray kept Mikki company at the moment.

She smiled, fighting her nerves to keep her voice cheerful for Mom and Mikki's sake. "Hey, Mikki. Dad, Ray? Can we talk in the hall a minute?" She stepped back and gripped Jack's hand.

He gave her an encouraging wince.

The puzzlement on Dad and Ray's faces slammed to anger the moment they saw Jack.

Ray took a threatening step forward. "Get the hell out of here, Jack." At least he kept his voice low.

"What are you doing here?" Dad folded his arms, glowering.

Cami clung to the firm anchor of Jack's hand. "Dad and Ray, stop it. I appreciate you wanting to protect me, but you're totally wrong about Jack. We need to end this crazy misunderstanding now."

Ray goggled at her. "Here? You're defending him? Are you nuts?"

"Yes. Here and now." She pushed past her anxiety. "Ray, you were wrong about Jack. You owe him a big apology."

"Ray? Dad? Cami, what's going on? Why are you all arguing out there?" Anxiety sharpened Mikki's voice.

Oh, boy, they hadn't kept their voices low enough.

Ray glanced over his shoulder, face torn with worry. "I'm coming, hon."

"Get in here now and tell me what's going on."

Cami sucked in her breath. Jack gave her an encouraging nod, and they stepped toward the door. Ray and Dad blocked them for a moment before backing inside.

"Jack, you're here too?" Mikki glanced from Cami to Jack and to their joined hands.

Mom set aside her embroidery. "Oh, my, Jack, your poor face. Were you in an accident?"

Mikki and Mom's puzzled but friendly welcome proved Ray and Dad hadn't filled them in on the morning's chaos.

Jack smiled and shrugged. "Hey, Mikki, sorry for intruding like this. Hi, Mrs. Alexander. Cami and I just needed to talk to Ray for a couple minutes."

"You're sorry. Yeah, right," Ray muttered as he went to Mikki's side.

Mikki pinned them all with a *don't mess with me stare*. "Okay, I'm hormonal, my back is killing me, and you have about five minutes before the next contraction hits to tell me what the heck is going on here. Why were you all arguing? Jack, what happened to your face?"

"Ray punched him." Cami shivered. Forgetting

the fright of this morning might take a while.

Mikki snapped her glare at Ray. "Ray, are you crazy?"

Ray scowled at Jack. "It really sucks I couldn't trust you with Cami."

"No, what really sucks is finding out my best friend believes I'm an asshole and won't give me a break to explain. That's real low, pal."

"Low? Low is you cheating on Cami and your girlfriend. Cami's like my sister! I can't believe you pulled this crap."

"Cami and you?" Mikki shrieked. "Girlfriend?"

Jack wrapped his arm possessively around Cami's waist. "Cami's my girlfriend. My *only* girlfriend. I've never cheated on anyone in my life."

"Cami, why didn't you say anything?" Mikki shook her head, her expression a mix of incredulous and stunned.

"Jack and I got together after the move, and the only woman he's been seeing is *me*. The secrecy was all my fault, not Jack's. You all were fussing so much over my dating life. I asked him to keep quiet about us, because I didn't want anyone to worry. We love each other, and we were going to come clean about our relationship as soon as Christie and Kaylie were born and life calmed down."

Ray narrowed his eyes at Jack, his face unforgiving. "You told me you were seeing someone."

"I am. I'm seeing *Cami*. I didn't want you fixing me up with a blind date, so I said as much as I could and still keep my promise to Cami."

Ray groaned, his shoulders slumping, and the flushed anger in his face plunged into deep shame.

"Oh, hell, I really screwed up. I believed you had a new girlfriend, then I saw you with Cami like that this morning. Mikki was in labor. I wasn't thinking. I just saw red. I'm sorry."

Jack held out his hand. "Since you were trying to protect Cami, you're forgiven." He winced. "Though I would have appreciated if you'd asked a few questions first."

Ray shook his hand. "I'm sorry. Real sorry. I should have known better."

"Timeout, guys. Oh—" Mikki's face constricted in pain, and Ray lunged to her side. "Stay!" Her gasped order froze everyone in place.

They waited in uncomfortable obedience as Mikki panted through the contraction, squeezing hard on Ray's hand.

Once Mikki had her breath again, she frowned at Cami. "You and Jack—You're serious? You're in love, and you haven't even been dating a month. That's too fast, Cami."

"I'm sure. I've wasted so much time trying to find the man I thought you all wanted for me, instead of looking for the man *I* wanted for me. I know better now. Jack's the man I love."

Jack smiled at Cami, love shining in his face. "No, our relationship has been completely the opposite of fast. We fell for each other six years ago, but we were both in relationships and never realized our connection went deeper than friendship. We've been good friends ever since, but as far as romance was concerned, we were two ships passing in the night."

Cami nodded. "Then, this fall, we were suddenly both free. Over the past few weeks we discovered we wanted to be far more than good friends." She turned to Jack. "I'm sorry it took so long for me to understand what I needed."

Jack brought her hand to his lips for a kiss. "I had plans to do this very differently, in a much more romantic setting, but it's time I make my feelings for you absolutely clear."

As he sank down onto one knee, he dug a hand in his jacket pocket and emerged with a sparkling ring.

Cami vaguely heard her family's shocked gasps as her own breath caught. He meant it *all*. He was doing this here, now?

"I love you, Cami. Every moment I'm with you is the best moment of my life. You're the one I want in my arms. You're the reason I can't wait to be home again when I'm at work. You're the only woman who's in my thoughts and fills my heart. No doubts. I love you, Cami. Always have and always will. Marry me. Please."

~*~

Jack waited, unable to breathe, his heart pounding. Please believe in us, Cami.

Tears filled her sweet brown eyes, and she threw her arms around him. "Yes. No more doubts. I love you, too."

His hands shook as he slipped the ring on Cami's finger. Dazed on a rush of joy and relief, he swept her into a hard kiss.

They parted from the kiss and stood, only to be greeted by commotion of the happy kind. Mrs. Alexander gave him a teary hug.

Ray shook his hand and clapped him on the shoulder. "I was an idiot. I'm happy for you two."

"Get over here, Jack, and let me hug you, you crazy guy," Mikki demanded.

He gave Mikki an awkward, gentle hug and kissed her cheek. Mikki and Cami threw their arms around each other.

"Oh, Cami, you're totally crazy, too, but I'm so happy for you." Mikki swiped tears from her cheeks.

He and Cami stepped aside to let Ray rejoin Mikki, but when they turned around, Mr. Alexander loomed in front of them, his face still stern. Then he offered his hand. Was that a shrewd twinkle and start of a smile softening his face?

"Welcome to the family, son. I expect you to take good care of my little girl."

Jack shook his hand. Making that promise was easy. "I will always do my best for Cami."

Mrs. Alexander wrapped her arm around her husband, and her smile sparkled. With her shock now past, she blissfully was embracing her role as the mother of the bride. "Of course, I know it's probably too soon for you two to have given wedding plans any thought, but do you have any ideas what you'd like?"

"It's up to Cami, but I don't see any need to wait." Sooner suited him just fine. He'd been ready for this next step since their first kiss, and the faster he made Cami his, the faster he could eliminate her last worries over their remaining secret.

He turned to her to find her smiling, peace and relief in place of the stress.

She squeezed his hand. "I know soon might seem kind of crazy, but I don't need a big showy wedding."

Mrs. Alexander narrowed her eyes at them both. "You two better drop any ideas of eloping right this minute. I want a proper wedding for Camille."

An idea struck Jack. "I have a thought. Your brother and his family are flying in the Saturday before Thanksgiving, on November twentieth, right? They'll be here two weeks. I remember you mentioned how hard it is for him to schedule time off from work. Why don't we try for November twenty-seventh, while they're here?"

Cami brightened. "That would be wonderful! Who knows when they'll be able to get back here again? Are you sure?"

"It works for me."

The idea of a wedding set only four weeks off sent Mrs. Alexander and Mikki into a tizzy, followed by more happy tears, interrupted by another contraction.

Timing-wise, planning even a simple, casual wedding was kind of crazy, with the NJEA convention, end of first marking period, and parent-teacher conferences all occurring within that time period. But if that's what Cami wanted, he'd make it happen.

Time came for Mikki to have another progress check, and the nurse chased them all but Ray from the room. They agreed to head downstairs to the coffee shop, where they ran into Ray's parents and Emily.

Jack called his parents and broke the news. Thankfully, they were too excited to question the fast wedding plans and thought making the accommodation for Cami's brother made total sense.

Next, Cami called her brother. Jack heard

Gerry's shocked "What!" loud and clear. The phone was passed around, and the conversations with Gerry and his wife were full of congratulations and questions.

By the time they'd finished eating, they had hashed out a preliminary plan, and the Thanksgiving week wedding was in motion.

They returned upstairs and shared the plans with Mikki and Ray. Mikki added in good ideas between contractions—which, she grumpily assured everyone, weren't even close to the real deal yet, and Ray should have let her stay home until now.

Oh, shit—Jack swallowed hard, caught in the unexpected sick riptide of worry. He might be going through this with Cami in July. He'd be in Ray's place, dealing with seeing Cami suffering, unable to make her pain go away. So much could go wrong . . . No wonder Ray had lost his mind and flipped out this morning.

Then he recalled the first time he saw Ray holding Emily. He remembered Ray's awestruck joy. A hot knot of emotion lodged in his chest. He might be holding his own daughter or son in July.

Eight o'clock arrived and the end of visiting hours. Mikki and the babies were doing very well, but while they looked good for a normal delivery, they had a long night ahead.

Mikki burst into tears. "I wish you all could stay. You were keeping me distracted."

Cami kissed Mikki. "You'll do great. Love you, sis. We'll see you tomorrow. "

"Love you, too."

Emily was asleep in Mr. Alexander's arms and slept through Mikki's teary goodnight kiss.

Mikki scrubbed at her tears and smiled tiredly at Jack. "Come here, Jack, and let me hug you. Take good care of my twin."

"I will." He leaned in close, and she hugged him hard.

Ray held out his hand. "Again, Jack, I'm real sorry I went off the deep end on you."

Jack shook his hand and clapped him on the back. "Forgiven. Good luck tonight to you both."

"Thanks. I'll keep you all posted when I can."

After another round of goodnight hugs outside in the parking lot, Ray's parents headed to their home. Mr. and Mrs. Alexander would stay at Mikki and Ray's with Emily.

On the drive home, Cami abruptly groaned, clapping a hand to her forehead. "I feel so bad, I can't believe I didn't even think—Mikki and Ray are counting on me living in the apartment. They need the rental income."

Jack smiled. He'd make sure to find them a new tenant. The apartment would work for a couple, and he'd heard Maxine Steiner and her husband were thinking of moving.

"I've already been considering that problem, and I may have friends who might be interested in your apartment. Maxine and Douglas Steiner. Nice folks. You've met them at a couple of my parties. His company moved down to Lakewood, and they're tired of the long commute from Edison. I can put them in touch with Ray."

"Oh, I remember them. That would be great, thanks."

After tucking Emily in bed, they were all still too wound up, so Cami made coffee and sliced up one of pies meant for the party, and they settled in to watching the World Series game and discussing how to handle the next day. They had Mikki and the babies to see and the party and trick or treaters to manage. Ray checked in around ten and midnight to let them know Mikki's labor was progressing and all was well.

Ray's final call came just after two in the morning. Jack was stretched out on the sofa with Cami drowsing in his arms, her dad was snoring in the recliner, and her mom was curled up on the love seat.

At the ring, Cami snapped upright. She fumbled the phone to speaker. "Ray?"

Her parents sat up blinking.

Ray's ebullient voice boomed over the speaker. "They're here. Perfect and beautiful and loud and healthy. Five pounds each. Wow, just wow. Mikki did awesome. Everything went great. I'm sending you photos."

"Congratulations. Love you all. Try to rest."

Ray laughed. "We'll crash hard soon. We'll see you tomorrow."

Soon her phone chirped again, delivering pictures of Ray and Mikki posing with beaming, exhausted smiles and tiny Kaylie and Christie in their arms.

"Oh, Jack, the girls are so beautiful." She curled her hand over Jack's.

Well, beautiful in that adorably ugly way only newborns could manage, with tiny, chubby-cheeked, scrunched red faces under their pink knit caps.

Would their child be as beautiful? Would their

child have Cami's eyes or his dark hair?

Rocked again by the realization that he was completely okay with the abrupt changes occurring in his life, Jack pulled Cami close for a hard kiss, elated and off-balance at no longer needing to hide his feelings.

After saying goodnight to Cami's parents, Cami and he headed to her place hand-in-hand.

At the foot of her stairs, she hugged Jack. "Stay tonight. Sleep here."

"I don't want to be anywhere else."

They tumbled exhausted into bed, and Jack gathered her into his arms with a kiss. "Goodnight. Love you."

"Love you too." She kissed him and curled her hand into his. "I meant to tell you earlier. I love the ring. It's perfect."

He brushed his fingers over the ring. She'd said yes!

"It was my grandmother's. I hoped you'd like it. She and my grandfather loved each other fiercely, and I can't think of a better way to mark the start of our life together."

~*~

Happy Halloween. Sort of.

Cami lay quietly, watching Jack as he slept, putting off the necessary trip to the bathroom and time of reckoning. She'd slept far better than she'd expected, considering how she'd dreaded this morning. Yesterday, she'd lost count of the emotional swings between which answer she wanted.

As for today? She pressed a hand to her belly. Today the second-guessing would be over, and she just had to deal with the answer. Only, would the answer be a trick or a treat?

What did she hope for when she wanted *both* answers?

Thanks to Jack, facing today was easier. She rubbed a finger over the slightly loose ring she now wore, not just any pretty ring picked at random, but his *grandmother's* ring, a poignant symbol promising she could trust in his friendship and in his love.

She slipped carefully from bed to avoid disturbing him. Her bare feet hit cold wood floor, and the chill tightened her stomach as she felt about for her slippers. She tiptoed to the bathroom and closed the door before turning on the light.

A minute later, she had an initial answer. Still no period. Would waiting another day for the test be better?

She poured a glass of water, washed her face, and brushed her hair.

No, the waiting, wondering, and crazy seesaw of emotions needed to be put to an end.

She retrieved the drugstore bag from under the sink. After a failed steadying breath, she followed the directions, and sat on the toilet to watch the clock on the vanity and wait for her answer. She couldn't look. She had to look.

A tap came at the door. "Cami?"

Sucking in a breath, she stood and opened the door.

Jack glanced from her to the tester sitting on the counter. "You okay?" His poor face was a bruised mess.

"I haven't looked yet." She bit her lip and glanced at the clock. "It's just time now."

"We started this together. We'll look together."

He wrapped his arms around her, and she folded her arms over his as they stepped over to the counter. He met her eyes in the mirror.

"No matter the answer, Cami. I love you."

"I love you, too."

"Then let's find out."

A mess of hopeful and terrified, Cami dragged in a shuddering breath, and looked.

A plus.

Shivers raced over her, her legs shook, shock and joy inseparable. Jack's arms tightened around her, and he carried her into his lap as he sank onto the toilet.

A plus.

Tears and breathless laughter sprang at the same time. She was going to be a mother.

"We're going to be a family." Jack was breathless also, but was that an *oh, crap* breathless or an *I'm okay with this* breathless?

She found her answer in his hard kiss, and his gentle thumbs brushing at her tears.

"Aw, Cami, don't cry. We're going to be okay." He crushed her close.

"Mostly happy tears. Are you okay?" She'd need to get it officially confirmed by her doctor, but she trusted this answer was real. Her emotions sprang into another crazy tumble and more tears spilled.

Chuckles rumbled through him. "Yes, more stunned than I expected and far happier than I hoped."

"You're happy? Really?"

"I am. How are you doing?"

"Happier and more terrified than I've ever been. I now know exactly the freaking-out, terrified, overjoyed feeling Mikki tried to explain."

"Freaking-out, terrified, overjoyed. Yep, that's the feeling in a nutshell." Jack spread his hand over her belly. "I love you, Cami, and I promise you, I'm going to love our baby, too."

"I love you." Those simple words were becoming easier and easier to say. A new dizzy wave rushed her. "Oh! What if there are two?" She'd avoided considering that possibility.

"More to love. And we have experts in the family for advice. We can do this." He kissed her and stood, scooping her up with him.

She laughed and threw her arms around him to hang on. "Where are we going?"

"Back to bed. I have a plan."

"You do, huh?"

"A very good one." He nuzzled sweet, tingling kisses over her as he carried her through the bedroom doorway.

"And what's in this plan?"

He set her softly on the bed. "I thought I'd start with some of these." He cupped her face and touched his mouth to hers, drawing her into a scorching kiss as he lay her back. "And show you over and over how much I love you.

The End

Thank You!

Thanks for reading *Convincing Cami*. I hope you enjoyed it!

Would you like to know when my next book is available? You can sign up for my e-mail list at http://www.babettejames.com/Newsletter.

You can also connect with me online at http://www.babettejames.com, follow me on Twitter http://twitter.com/BabetteJames, or like my Facebook page http://facebook.com/BabetteJamesAuthor.

I would appreciate it if you would help others enjoy this book, too.

Recommend it. Please help other readers find this book by recommending it to friends, readers' groups and discussion boards.

Review it. Reviews help readers find books and I appreciate all reviews.

You've just read the second book in my His Girl Next Door Series. The other books in the series are *Kissing Katie* (Available now), *Tempting Tessa* (Coming 2015), and *Loving Lexi* (Coming 2015). I hope you enjoy them all!

Coming Soon

Here's an excerpt of TEMPTING TESSA, Book 3 in the His Girl Next Door Series by Babette James.

Coming February 2015

Ever since Tessa Wainwright moved into the rundown bungalow next door, Hale Lindstrom has been captivated by the smart and lovely college student. His busy plumbing business helps him keep a responsible distance, but she seems alone in the world, so he lends a hand when he can. His plan works fine, until he accidentally hits her with a snowball and learns she isn't the kid he assumed. Their tumble into love brings happiness, but he's got a secret he's determined to conceal from Tessa at all costs.

After frustrating years of planning and saving, Tessa is pursuing her dream of a literature degree. Shy, sexy Hale is a serious temptation, but her goals leave no room for romance and she's done with men trying to fix her life. Despite her resolve, a polar vortex, a goofy dog, and an irresistible guy are rewriting her carefully outlined future. Maybe falling in love is an unavoidable plot twist, but Hale's refusal to trust may doom their hopes of a happy ending.

AS THEY REACHED HER DRIVEWAY, HALE TURNED. "Hey, Tessa? Ah, want some coffee?"

His hopeful smile completely erased Tessa's intention to return to her writing. "Sounds good."

Honks filled the air as a V formation of geese strafed low overhead, aiming for the marsh.

Geese. Oh, no!

Hale lunged for Gunner's collar. "Gunner! No!"

With a joyful woof, Gunner charged after the flock, yanking Hale into a skid over the icy driveway before the collar ripped from Hale's gloved hand. Scrambling for traction, Hale rammed into Tessa, and they crashed into the snowdrift.

Thank goodness for the still mostly fluffy snow. Squished, but unhurt, Tessa looked up at Hale, catching her breath from the jarring fall and his big body crushing her into the snow. Happy barks and peeved honks grew rapidly distant. Rushing breaths mixed in steamy clouds.

His mouth was so close. Every imprint of Hale's body against hers was suddenly clear despite their heavy winter clothes, the intimate weight of him against her outrageously wonderful, luxurious.

"Damned dopey dog—"

She saw the exact instant Hale's exasperation flashed into desire and those clear blue eyes glittered with passion.

Yes, please, kiss me.

Heat pooled in her belly and rushed over her skin, overwhelming her with reckless need.

Kiss me, kiss me, I don't care if it's crazy or foolish, just kiss me.

He did.

His mouth was shockingly warm, his lips strong and soft. This was the fiery kiss promised in the banked warmth of their shy New Year's Eve kiss. This was the kiss she'd yearned for in her dreams. Better.

Bundled as they were against the cold, they explored all that bare faces, mouths, lips, and tongues could invent and combine. He delved gloved hands beneath her hood and gripped her head as his mouth possessed hers in the lovely, lovely insanity.

Hot, intense, almost alarming—she had to shut her eyes against the deluge of sensation: the faint salty taste of him, his warm outdoorsy scent, the fine grit and rasp of his beard, his hot, wet mouth, the drugging thrust of his tongue, his sharp nips, and soothing licks. Clutching his jacket, she wriggled greedily for more contact, moaning in the pleasure as he settled between her legs and his hard arousal met her center.

Ah, you know, you're seriously making out in the front yard. Anyone might drive by and see.

Did she care? Not one bit.

~*~

Available Now

Here's an excerpt of SUMMERTIME DREAM, Book 1 in The River Series by Babette James.

The Fourth of July is over, but for these summer lovers, the fireworks have just begun.

An unexpected inheritance brings business consultant Christopher Gordon from Los Angeles to quaint Falk's Bend. He's carved time from his demanding schedule to dispose of his great-grandparents' home and explore his roots. However, disturbing family secrets and the sweet temptation of writer Margie Olsson derail his plans, challenging him to seize the elusive dream missing from his hectic life—love.

A recent brush with death shook Margie's life, but not her dreams, and she's ready to move forward. Only, standing up to her loving, over-protective family isn't easy. Helping Christopher explore the derelict mansion and unravel his grandmother's mysterious past allows a fun taste of independence. But when her experimental summer fling ignites into unexpected love, can her small town dreams work with his big city life?

THE FOURTH OF JULY IN FALK'S BEND, Missouri, made pretending nothing ever changed almost possible, Margie Olsson decided. All it took was a dollop of stiff determination and a generous application of wishful thinking.

Even the arguments remained the same.

"Told you we'd be late." Her brother Joe wrenched open the hatch to their restaurant's minivan, the tight muscle in his jaw sending his mustache twitching.

Most of the townsfolk had finished migrating from the parade route to River Edge Park and claimed their favorite picnic table or stretch of ground. Now they swarmed the softball field and concession stand, ready to enjoy the town's 132nd annual Independence Day game.

Unperturbed at Joe's grouching, Dad hefted the massive pan of beans. "Why rush to sit and stew in a long line of cars? It's not like anyone would take our table. Plus, we can take our time unloading." With that, he trundled off to the large brick grills.

Joe's frown sharpened into a scowl that would do one of their Viking ancestors proud. "We could always try getting here early!" he growled at Dad's back and dragged out the largest ice chest.

Margie choked off a laugh. Some things had remained absolute over her twenty-four years of life: Dad would never arrive early to any event and Joe would always fuss like a mother hen.

"At least you have a sunny day for the game." She patted Joe's shoulder. "Cooler than last week, don't you think? I don't think we've had a more sweltering end of June."

Joe nodded woodenly. "I got the rest. Go on and find Grandma and Grandpa. Looks like Mom got them here on time." He waved her off, as if she were still a preschooler tagging her heels. This, with his being ten years older, was a familiar feeling.

As soon as he turned his back, Margie scooped up the smallest ice chest and followed him to their table where Grandpa and Grandma Olsson's wicker picnic basket waited.

Unfortunately, facts trumped determination and wishful thinking. Not everything in Falk's Bend remained the same. The Heller family's traditional table stood conspicuously empty, as did the Frost family's table. Being spared the inevitable awkward encounters should be a relief, but the gossips would surely set to talking again, and the misery flashing over Joe's face lodged a knot in her throat.

She fell in beside him as he returned for the next load. Should she ask now? The timing wasn't perfect, but she had him alone. A glance over to Dad found him gabbing with the four elderly Mills brothers, who thrived on checkers and gossip while supervising the assorted dishes simmering on the grills. Over at the gate, a tall man in a white shirt paused, and rubbed the back of his neck as he scanned the confusion of tables, until Bert Mills hailed him over. They all shook hands like old friends, so maybe he was the grandnephew expected down from Montana.

Margie blew at her bangs. Cooler weather was debatable. The heavy air clung like a steamy second skin and the flags, bunting, and bows draped the park as perky as wet laundry.

"Hey, Joe, I was thinking, I'd really like to get back to work on Monday." She winced at her blurt. Although Aunt Ida handled the staff schedules and Dad was the official boss, Joe ruled the family's restaurant these days and he'd be the hardest nut to crack in her effort to return to normal life.

"Aw, Margie, we agreed you'd use the time to rest up and write and start when Amy headed back to school in August."

"Come on. At least part time. I'm totally fine

now. I miss working—" She stumbled over a rough grass tuft.

Joe steadied her, his face strained and gaze darting over her. "You all right, sweetie? Maybe you should just take it easy today."

Oh, that snapped her last straw. "I'm fine! I'm weary to pieces with hearing 'Take it easy.' Dr. Saylor said no restrictions. I can do what I want. When I want. Anything!"

"Hey, Margie? Joe?" Her best friends Debi and Baxter strolled up beside Joe.

Joe planted his hands on his hips, another lecture looming. "Margie, I know, but—"

She crossed her arms against the chill surge of shame at losing her temper in public and her throat tightened. "No! Enough! You've got work to do. I'll see you after the game."

Grumbling under his breath, Joe stomped off.

Baxter dropped his bag on the table and stooped to kiss Debi quick and hard. "Hon, I'll go on help Joe unload. See you at the bleachers." He winked at Margie and loped after Joe.

Mirth sparkling in her blue eyes, Debi hugged Margie. "Well, well, there's hope for you after all! I've never seen you back Joe down before."

"He's just . . . being Joe. I shouldn't have snapped at him." Margie groaned. The giddy spark at having stood up for herself fizzled. Thank goodness, her parents had missed her tantrum. Joe hadn't been himself since breaking up with Stephanie and jumping down his throat was a dumb way to get his agreement.

"I've known you since the first day of kindergarten, and yeah, Joe means well, but let me tell you, that was one long overdue snap. I'm proud of you."

"I just wish he'd stop hovering." Margie peeked over her shoulder at the minivan. Baxter had Joe's softball gear, and Joe hauled out the first large, food-laden hotbox.

"Maybe you ought to think about a place of your own. You need a change."

"I've had enough change over the last year."

Debi waved her hand in a stop-it motion. "A positive change. And, yes, I know all the reasons why you stay with them. Heck, I'd leave Baxter for your mom's peach pancakes alone. But it's something you should consider seriously."

"I will. Someday." Even moving out wouldn't stop their loving, smothering concern.

"Why don't we skip the game? I'll crack open the pinot grigio and we can compare brotherly pet peeves."

Margie laughed. "I think we've covered them all over the years. Go on. Catch up with Baxter. Let me jot some quick scene notes, then I'll meet up with you all." That was a complete fib, but her skin crawled with the need for some space.

Debi accepted her fib with a commiserating hug and headed for the ball field.

Margie escaped for her favorite place in the park, the huge old oak topping the low rise of land between the picnic area and the ball field, with a perfect view of the game and the lazy river. Oh, thank goodness, she had the shady homemade swing to herself. She settled against the swing's thick rope, kicked off her sandals, and let out a heavy breath. Two sparrows squabbled and chased overhead through the shifting patterns of leafy shadow and sunlight. Drawing her bare feet up onto the heavy board polished smooth by years of bottoms and feet, she fluffed the skirt of her sundress over her knees. Determined to change her fib and mood around, she opened the story on her tablet and set to her note-making, resisting the urge to aimlessly edit.

Wild cheers jolted her attention to the game. Whoa. Seven innings already and tied at nine runs each. She sighed. Her missing the game would just give Joe one more thing to fuss over.

They all meant well, but when would Joe and everyone accept she was perfectly fine, better than ever, actually, and stop trying to keep her packed in cotton balls?

Patience, patience. All you can do is wait.

"Wait for what?" a quiet male voice answered.

Jolted, she sat straight, straddling the board to keep from falling, her heart zipping. She'd spoken out loud?

"Sorry, didn't mean to startle you." The man from the gate stood at the edge of the shade. "Just came over to check out this great old oak. I'll leave you be."

His soft, low voice, rich and warm as caramel, set every dormant feminine nerve on alert.

But who was he? Between growing up in Falk's Bend and working at the restaurant, she knew everyone and their kin, or, at least about them. If he was a Mills, he must take after his mother's family. He had the greenest eyes she'd ever seen set in a craggy, captivating face, and smile crinkles by his eyes and mouth. He was lanky and fit, but not so tall as Joe, and maybe older, late thirties. His sleek brown hair was neatly trimmed, his white polo shirt set off his outdoor tan, and more men should look as good in jeans as he did. Her gaze returned to those remarkable eyes of his, and something hot and bright leapt inside her.

He cleared his throat, as if he'd been waiting for a reply.

Holy moly. Heat flooded her. She'd been staring like an idiot. So that's what all that being lost in a man's eyes in romance novels felt like. Holy moly indeed.

~*~

Available Now

Here's an excerpt of CLEAR AS DAY, Book 2 in The River Series by Babette James.

What's a girl to do when her summer lover wants forever?

Haunted by dark memories of her parents' volatile marriage, artist Kay Browning keeps her heart locked behind a free-spirit facade and contents herself with the comfortable affair she has every summer with easygoing photographer Nate Quinn.

The only trouble with her plan? This summer Nate's come to Lake Mohave to claim the lover he can't let go. He's done with the endless traveling and settling for temporary homes and temporary loves. Kay's always been more than just a vacation fling, and now he must convince this woman, who sees love as a course to certain heartbreak, to take that leap of faith and learn how safe love with the right man can be.

OF COURSE, THE MORE SHE DETERMINED NOT TO think of Nate, the more she did.

"Just perfect." Kay Browning tipped her Dodgers cap low against the mid-morning glare and kicked into a hard backstroke through the cool water. Blue skies, hot July sun, intense desert landscape—another perfect day at Lake Mohave. Except for the futile if-onlys snarled in her mind like fishing line.

Nate Quinn had come along with July and Mohave for the past six years. He'd sail in like a freshening wind, they'd share two weeks of fishing, playing, and loving, Kay's careful schedule demolished to a pleasant shambles, and then he'd be off again on his adventures. Kay's life would resume its organized pace, punctuated by glossy postcards, scattered bursts of e-mails, IMs and silly tweets, the occasional twenty-plus-page letter, and the odd oblivious-to-time-zone phone call.

Kay liked how they kept the relationship simple. No demands on each other. No clinging, pining or carping. A happy, mutual understanding: she stayed and he went. But this summer, however much she hated admitting the feeling, Nate's absence threw off her sense of balance.

No whining, no pining, remember? She turned with a splash, adjusted her cap, and swam hard toward shore.

Life happens. Focus on what you can control.

At the moment, that was her painting.

She allowed herself one heavy sigh. Why every last one of her friends had inexplicably cancelled on the set-in-stone annual vacation—well, plans change. As for Nate . . . She hadn't pined over anything since she was ten. This was simple, annoying regret.

She coasted into the shallows, rolled to her back and forced herself to relax and float. In her mind's eye she drew Nate sitting there on the beach with the sun-drenched background of stark rocky land and softening tangles of willow, mesquite, and tamarisk, and the mental exercise halfway worked in distracting the fidgets—as long as she kept her eyes closed. Fantasizing wasn't pining. Quick pencil strokes to block him in. Slower, surer on the details. He liked his blond hair in a crew cut. His lean shoulders, strong, long hands . . . She trailed her fingertips over his favorite path from her waist over her ribs upward to—Nope, no fantasizing that way. Back to drawing. Maybe she'd grab a sketchpad later and work out a few real drafts.

Lips set together, relaxed, with the faintest lift of a smile at the corners. The faint crook to his rugby-broken nose. His agile, comic eyebrows lay thick and straight over gray eyes. His ears stuck out a charming slightest bit. Beautiful cut abs and pecs proved his claims of laziness a lie. A perfect amount of body hair dusted silky crisp over chest, arms and legs. Men were such texture contrasts: the satin of skin and rasp of hair, jut of bone and arc of muscle, soft lips and calloused fingers. He wouldn't have shaved yet today, and there would have been sandpapery-rough morning kisses. She almost heard him calling her, "Hey, Kay!" in the relaxed, husky way he—

With a splash, she erased the frustrating daydream. This wishful imagining fixed nothing. Her sheltered little camp would still be empty. Should she give in, pack up the camp, and hit the road north to Lake Mead instead? Just break her routine for once.

No, but it was definitely past time to get her tush out of the water and do something constructive. This lonely gnawing in her bones and brain was unacceptable. Kay pushed to her feet, facing out to the scenic lake created out of a stretch of the Colorado River and the rugged land beyond shimmering with heat.

Work, right, but it was too early in the day for the hard afternoon light she needed for the Coyote

Point painting. She was too restless to read or fish and not in the mood to take the boat over to the marina, chat with George, and buy ice.

She rolled her shoulders and stretched, enjoying the hot air licking over her wet skin. As she wiggled her feet in the sand and gravel-bottomed shallows, a flurry of minnows darted past her ankles, and her silver toe ring glinted beneath the clear water. She paused, caught by the possibilities in the sparkling sun on water and the intricate, shifting reflections over gravel. Yes! Exactly the distracting challenge she needed. Shaking the water from her ears, she pivoted toward camp.

"Kay!" That male voice was not her imagination.

"Oh, shit!" She twisted and dropped into the water, sinking neck-deep. Mother always said, among other things, that a lady never goes skinny-dipping and must always wear a proper hat. Kay was only half skinny-dipping, but she fervently wished she'd worn something a bit more substantial than a baseball cap and the bottom half of the quintessential teeny-weenie yellow polka-dot bikini.

Shit, oh, shit, oh, shit. She so hated when Mother was right.

Okay, time to find out who'd just gotten an eyeful. The guy had called her name, so she should know him. Oh boy, if she'd flashed old George . . .

She wiped water from her face, sucked in a breath against her pounding heart, and peeked around.

Nate.

She must be sun-dazed. Nate? With a beard? Hair curling over his ears? No way. Just because a familiar slouchy fishing hat topped those unruly, sun-bleached blond curls and just because this guy possessed the same deep-water tan and footloose taste in clothes as Nate with his electric blue Hawaiian shirt, bright orange swim trunks, and beat-up deck shoes didn't mean—

"Hey, babe. Now that I've finally caught your attention, how about a hug from my girl?" He opened his arms. "Am I coming in after you or are you coming out?" Only Nate's voice held that mellow timbre like chocolate for her ears.

"Nate! What…" Giddy delight flushed over Kay, clearing her shock. She dashed from the water and into strong arms, a wonderful hug, and a better kiss that launched her mind into a blissed-out whirl of *oh, yes* and *why*?

The *oh, yes* won out until the need to breathe forced them apart.

Nate gave her a long look, his usually easy gray eyes holding a new, simmering heat.

Wow. Whoa.

His slow hands followed the trail of his roving gaze: gentle tracing of cheek and lips, gliding across hips, waist and ribs, and grazing over her breasts to cup and caress. With his tender, simple touches, he stirred the warm desire of her daydream into full need. She shut her eyes, soaking in the unexpected pleasure. *Oh, yes.*

~*~

About the Author

Babette James writes sweetly scorching contemporary romance and loves reading nail-biting tales with a satisfying happily ever after. When not dreaming up stories, she enjoys playing with new bread recipes and dabbling with paints. Babette is a member of New Jersey Romance Writers, Romance Writers of America, Contemporary Romance Writers, Celtic Hearts Romance Writers, and Liberty States Fiction Writers. As a teacher, she loves encouraging new readers and writers as they discover their growing abilities. Her class cheers when it's time for their spelling test! Born in New Jersey and raised in Southern California, she's had a life-long love of the desert and going down the shore. Babette lives in New Jersey with her wonderfully patient husband and extremely spoiled cats.

www.ingramcontent.com/pod-product-compliance
Lightning Source LLC
Chambersburg PA
CBHW070843120626
46556CB00002B/860